The Case of Sonia Wayward

The Case of
Sonia Wayward

MICHAEL INNES

Dodd, Mead & Company

NEW YORK

Published by Dodd, Mead & Company, Inc.
79 Madison Avenue, New York, N.Y. 10016

Distributed in Canada by
McClelland and Stewart Limited, Toronto

Manufactured in the United States of America

First Red Badge printing

Library of Congress Catalog Card Number: 60-11933
ISBN: 0-396-08343-9

Quotation from the "Ode to Music" by Robert Bridges
reproduced by permission of the Clarendon Press,
Oxford, England

Contents

I

Colonel Petticate
at Sea

I

Colonel Petticate stared at his wife in stupefaction. He could scarcely believe the evidence of his eyes—or of the fingers which he had just lifted from her pulse. But it was true. The poor old girl was dead.

Colonel Petticate gave a long whistle. It was the sort of whistle that indicates a consciousness, on the whistler's part, that here is a facer or a rum go. So it couldn't be regarded as a decorous—or at least adequate—comment on his discovery. But then, at the moment, Colonel Petticate was entirely alone.

This had not been true five minutes earlier. Then, there had been Sonia, bustling energetically around the confined space that had, during this holiday, exacerbated their normal state of mild conjugal irritation. Now, there was no Sonia; there was only this slumped and inert object . . . Colonel Petticate looked again at the body. As he did so, he became conscious that he was feeling queasy. This, like the whistle, was surely a queer reaction to what had so suddenly happened. Could it be that he was merely seasick? Their little yacht—now *his* little yacht—was certainly pitching a bit at anchor. But of course he was a seasoned sailor, so there could be nothing in that. No—he was feeling queasy merely because he was very frightened. Sonia had let him down. She had so contrived matters that she herself was without a care in the world—in any world that Colonel Petticate was at all disposed to believe in. But what the devil was to become of him?

Petticate pulled himself together and took further steps to assure himself that his wife was really dead. Since he was a retired army surgeon, he didn't feel that there was any difficulty about that. Then he sat down by the tiller and stared at the waters of the English Channel, silvery in the evening light. But the waters had nothing to say to him. Their neutrality and indifference were absolute. The death of Mrs. Ffolliot Petticate (as poor Sonia had occasionally condescended to be styled in private life) was no affair of theirs. If he had strangled her, or hit her on the head with the boat hook, their disinterest would still have been as entire. But Sonia's death had been wholly natural. If it seemed monstrously *not* natural, it was its very naturalness that gave it that effect. Murder is natural enough; in the jungle, which is more or less the state of nature, it keeps on happening. Suicide is natural—at least to the extent that nothing can be more sensible than suicide in this shattering world. But *this* was as unnatural as anything insolently inexplicable must always appear to the obstinately rational human mind.

Petticate himself was eminently rational. He noticed that, although the shock of the thing had been terrific, he had no impulse to mourn for Sonia. For a moment this made him feel rather callous. But then he remembered having read that mourning for the dead takes its origin in suppressed impulses of hostility, and is in fact a sort of death wish. So his failure to feel grief was perhaps a tribute to the decent

[4]

tolerance which he had managed for years to feel towards his wife.

This reflection ought to have been a tranquilizing one. But, oddly enough, it made Petticate even more uneasy. He got up and moved shakily into the cabin. On the ingenious little stove were the sauté potatoes Sonia had already prepared, and beside them were four chops waiting to be grilled. He supposed that he could eat four chops, once his stomach had got over its bad turn. But it might be better to keep two for tomorrow. After all, tomorrow was the rub. Or if not tomorrow, then the day after—and all the days after that. For he and Sonia had always spent, quarter by quarter, whatever came in. Sonia had seen a fine artistic improvidence as part of her role. He hadn't minded. It had never occurred to him that he would be the survivor.

What had carried her off, of course, was some circulatory catastrophe. Probably it was an embolism; indeed there was no other explanation. A hale and hearty woman, perfectly fit to haul up an anchor. But it was while hauling up the anchor that she had dropped. Yes, embolism was what the post-mortem would show. Or was aneurysm the word he wanted? He had gone rusty on these things since the early retirement that had followed his marriage.

The yacht pitched, and a slipper with an absurd fluffy pompon slid across the floor. He almost called out to Sonia some jaded pleasantry about tidiness on shipboard. She wasn't a tidy woman. The little table forrard was littered with typescript, and there was a further silt of the stuff on the floor. From the portable typewriter a final sheet protruded. He walked over to it and looked at the last word. It was "inchoate"—which meant that the next word, the word she would never type, ought to be "eyes." "He looked at her out of fathomless inchoate eyes." The sentence would be something like that. As a young woman she had picked up a vocabulary from D. H. Lawrence, and she had applied it to her own somewhat different literary purposes ever since. Colonel Petticate stirred some of the littered sheets contemptuously with a toe. *Opera interrupta* he said to himself, quoting a writer for whom he had rather more esteem.

It was undeniable that Ffolliot Petticate, although so rational a man, had allowed his settled attitude to his wife to be largely determined by a purely emotional occasion. At first he had been rather pleased with her. It was amusing to be married to a celebrity. And she was certainly a celebrity of sorts. The name of Sonia Wayward was a household word. If the households of which this held true scarcely included those of the most intellectual bent or ripest literary cultivation, it was at least a fact that Sonia's romances had earned the regard of gratifyingly large sections of the public alike in England and America. This meant that she earned a lot of money. And these were circumstances which Petticate found entirely agreeable. Sonia's wasn't a sort of reputation that need make an intelligent and sophisticated husband feel cast into the shade; and when he did grow a little tired of it he had the resource of a small society of cronies with whom he could share an attitude of civilized irony towards the whole affair. Moreover Sonia was really very amusing. She was genuinely the possessor of temperament—which in certain moods she would fling about in the interest of a jollity that was, somehow, catching. If Petticate himself never quite caught it, he didn't for a long time—surprisingly enough—at all resent it whizzing round his ears.

He had formed his own picture of his position in their circle: a man inevitably, because of his intellectual attainments, a little aloof, but nevertheless courteous and even cordial in his quiet well-bred way. When Sonia described one of her male characters as spare and distinguished, and endowed him with impressive if vague aristocratic associations, Colonel Petticate always supposed that she was taking the wifely liberty of exploiting him for the purpose of a little "copy." This made the actual disillusioning incident all the more disconcerting.

It was a matter of overhearing something she said on the telephone. There was nothing out of the way in his doing this. Sonia talked so loudly, whether on the telephone or off it, that it was inevitable he should hear a great deal that was not directly addressed to him. It had come about, indeed, that he was thus often unaware whether he was overhearing her or not. A particular remark would catch his attention, and then he might consciously listen until he grew tired of it. This was what happened on the fatal occasion.

"But, *darling*, you simply *must* meet my husband!"

She was talking, he had vaguely registered, to someone she hadn't seen for twenty years—a circumstance which naturally made her all the more breathlessly ardent in tone. So he had listened, amused and rather gratified.

"But you must, you *must*. Come to luncheon, come to dinner. I can guarantee that Ffolliot will be there. He never, *never* misses a meal. And he's the quaintest little creature in the world!"

It was quite clear to Colonel Petticate afterwards that what had shocked him about this performance was its sheer bad form. It was *that* which he had never quite managed to forgive. He hadn't—he found as he sat in the little cabin, with Sonia's body in the open stern behind him—forgiven it yet.

Nevertheless he was only halfway through his first chop when he found that he was weeping. It was his brief tribute to his honest consciousness that she hadn't been a bad sort. But it was connected, too, with the fact that he didn't now feel less frightened than he had done when the thing happened. And being thus instinctively frightened induced in him, at another level of his mind, a sort of wary and reasonable alarm. It was clear to him that he had become pretty dependent on Sonia—and perhaps not merely on account of her being the bread-and-butter, as well as the caviar and champagne. He must get rid of his dependence. In fact, he must get rid of *her*.

What he had already got rid of—and all within the hour —was the better part of a bottle of whisky. There was nothing much to that. He was accustomed to knowing just where he stood—or at least just how he lay—when in liquor. It therefore never got him into situations unbecoming a gentleman, as he conceived that becomingness. Which made it strange that the whisky betrayed him now. He was aware that he had a good deal to think about, but less clear that what was now going on in his head was ceasing to be thinking in any very strict sense. The element of rational apprehensiveness in his dismay progressively sank beneath something merely muddled. Presently he was telling himself that he was confronted with a terrible nuisance, a really intolerable bother. What happened when you sailed into port with a dead body? He didn't at all know—but he was quite sure that the formalities would be extremely vexatious. And just when he had so unmistakably had enough of

Sonia! With a flicker of sanity he pushed away the whisky bottle. But it wasn't before he had had his brilliant idea. Why not just lose Sonia overboard?

He went aft again and stood beside the body. It was dusk and he must do something about his riding light. But there wasn't a sail in sight. Any action he was minded to take, he could take in utter secrecy. He bent over the body. It was still quite flexible. He had forgotten how heavy they were —dead bodies. Or was the difficulty something to do with that whisky? He struggled, and something ripped in his hand. It was only the linen shirt beneath her jersey. But it gave him a new idea. Or rather it stirred in him an obscure consciousness that somewhere in his mind there lurked an idea he hadn't yet managed to haul up and look at. Surely it would be better . . .

He prowled about the little craft, trying to think what it was that he knew would be better—better than tipping Sonia over the side just as she was. He was unsteady now on his feet, and when going forward he stumbled and was aware of something flapping round his head. He reached up blindly, and found that he had grabbed her bathing costume, where it hung up to dry. That was it—if only he could manage it. If he could get the clothes off her, and her body into this. He took down the costume and then hesitated, confusedly aware of an obstacle that wasn't just the physical difficulty. A vast horror rose for a moment in his mind—and then blew away as if the chill evening wind had taken it. He went aft and knelt down beside the body. It wasn't hard to strip. He knew where the zips and fasteners were. But the next stage was more laborious. The bathing costume was damp still. That didn't help. Halfway through, he stopped and tried to close her eyes. Perhaps, he thought,

[9]

it was old professional instinct. Or perhaps he didn't like them. Perhaps they were still looking at the quaintest little creature in the world.

But she went in and down with hardly a ripple. Once he had got her over the side—which was a struggle—she just sank, lost form, vanished. He had been intent on the job, secure in his solitude. He had been so secure, indeed, that he had failed to notice that it was no longer solitude, after all. He had got her over the port gunwale; he turned to starboard—and there was another little yacht, no distance away. He was gripped by horrible fear—fear that took him and unmanned him, so that he could hardly stumble into the cabin before his knees gave way and he was on the floor. He lay for a long time shivering, expecting to hear a hail, or even the sound of the other craft coming alongside. But there was no sound but the faint lapping of the water against the shell of his own yacht. Even that terrified him. It sounded like somebody tapping. It sounded like *her*. . . .

Nothing happened. He got up and peered out—first warily through the little porthole, and then from out in the open. The other yacht had grown small in the distance. Of course he hadn't been discovered. But it had been a near thing. Lucky he had chosen the port side. He had been careless, of course, not to take a good look round. And one can't afford to be careless.

Petticate paused, frowning. Why had he said that to himself? It was the sort of thing a fellow said when engaged in a piece of wrongdoing, even in a crime. He himself wasn't in the least involved in anything of *that* sort. He had simply been taking a modern, strictly rational view of the sensible way of disposing of a dead body. It might offend old-fashioned sensibilities. There were still people who were shocked if you didn't wear mourning. And no doubt if the undertakers got hold of the matter, they might feel done out of a job. But of course he had acted entirely within his rights. He was more than three miles out at sea—decidedly in international waters. And he was captain or master or whatever it was called of this particular craft. It was entirely for him to decide for or against burial at sea. It would have been a shade more regular, perhaps, if he had read the appropriate parson's piece. But that wasn't among such literature as the yacht carried.

It was almost dark, and he busied himself with his light. He had no fancy for being run down by a liner. If he was to drown, he would, somehow, like it to be in another part of the ocean. And something was puzzling him. He tried to remember what it was. Yes—of course. Why had he put Sonia into that bathing costume? It didn't seem to hitch on to burial at sea. He must have had something else in mind. And if he could only recall what it was, then things would be more comfortable.

In great perplexity, Petticate wandered back into the cabin. There was, he seemed to remember, some whisky somewhere. A dash of that might serve to clear his head. But now he couldn't find the whisky. The bottle, although it was straight in front of his thin and rather handsome nose, somehow eluded him. He sat down wearily and listened again to the lapping. This time he connected it with nothing in particular—except with hearing it, night by night, as he went to sleep. Yes, it was a pleasant drowsy sound.

He woke up to darkness, and to cold and cramp. Something was digging into his side. But for a moment he didn't attend to that, since his mind was wholly occupied with some inexplicable sense of horror. He called out incoherently to his wife, but she didn't answer him. Then he knew that an irrevocable thing had happened. That was why he was sitting here, with the little folding table digging into him, instead of lying in his bunk. He had done something gratuitous and wanton, something with no reasonable sense to it. He sat up, and the movement put him abruptly in possession of the whole thing. What he had done had been not merely irrational. It had been fearfully dangerous as well. For no conceivable advantage, he was committed to telling a thumping lie—to swearing that Sonia had vanished while swimming from the side of the yacht. Of course she might have had her fatal attack while in the water, so that even if her body were recovered—as it well might be—he would probably be all right after all. Provided, that was to say, that nobody on that other yacht began to remember seeing anything odd.

Petticate got to his feet and lit the lamp, pumping clumsily and cautiously to get the pressure right. Then he moved about the cabin uneasily, conscious that there was something he had to find. But what he had to find was really inside his own head—something that was somehow going to lift a great burden, a great shame, from his mind. His foot slipped on paper, and he found himself looking down at the litter of typescript on the floor. Next, he stared at the typewriter—stared at it with narrowed apprehensive eyes, as if it might begin to clatter of itself. He didn't much like what it was accustomed to produce. Yet he had lived on it for years. The click of its keys had been the same as the clink of the coins in his pocket; the rustle of its carbon paper and its quarto sheets had merged with the crinkle of bank notes in his wallet.

Then, quite suddenly, Petticate had a sensation of standing amid blinding light. The effect was purely psychological, since there was now in the cabin a very good light already. He squared his shoulders. He put up his chin. The muscles round his mouth relaxed. If he had been challenged at that moment by some recording angel, he would have declared that Ffolliot Petticate, M.B., R.A.M.S. (retired), was an honest man again. For he had, after all, done nothing that betrayed the noble rationality of the creed by which he lived.

He sat down before the machine. He tapped out a single word. Then he read the completed sentence. His guess, he found, hadn't been a bad one. The sentence read:

There was that which was at once inscrutable and inchoate in eyes.

He looked back at the previous sentence and got his bearings. Then he tapped again, pausing only to locate the shift key, so that he produced:

There was that which was at once inscrutable and inchoate in his eyes.

It didn't mean a thing. But that, of course, was just as it should be. To hell with the *opera* being *interrupta*. Business As Usual was to be his motto henceforth. He was sure that Sonia would have wanted just that.

2

"I've read the first thirty thousand words," Petticate said. "Quite charming. Sonia at her best. And you know—you and I know, my dear man—just what *that* means."

He was sitting in the office of Sonia's publisher, Ambrose Wedge. It was an extremely shabby office. It had been an extremely shabby office ever since the day Ambrose Wedge's father had opened it—buying up for the purpose the entire *mise en scène* of a decayed and obscurely disgraced late-Victorian solicitor. By this simple means Ambrose Wedge's father successfully created the impression that Wedges had been prominent pretty well at the birth of English publishing—finding the poet Milton, perhaps, that risky ten pounds for *Paradise Lost,* or extending timely aid to the genteel indigence of Fielding or Steele. The solicitor's black-japanned deed-boxes remained ranged round the walls, with the names of the old clients erased and new ones painted in—this in a paint so obtrusively yellowed by age that one rather expected to read among them *Miss Emily Brontë* or *William Wordsworth, Esquire* or even just *The Author of Waverley*. Among the actual names, such as they were, *Sonia Wayward* held an honourable prominence. Petticate, indeed, was regarding it complacently now. *Executors of Sonia Wayward,* he was reflecting, wouldn't look nearly so nice.

"Sonia at her best?" Wedge—who was in fact a man of curiously pyramidal structure—tilted back comfortably in his swivel chair. "But when, bless her heart, is she anything else? It's always a pleasure to see the new Sonia Wayward in the bookshops. Don't you agree?"

"I do."

Petticate spoke with conviction. Perhaps because he had been constrained to tell so many lies of late, he was emphatic where ever his sincerity could be unflawed.

"Never tires."

"Never. This new book is entirely fresh."

"Fresh?" A shade of misgiving, even of alarm, spread over Wedge's features. "She's not breaking new ground?"

"No, no—nothing of the sort." Petticate hastily clarified his statement. "I mean merely that the writing has a wonderful quality of freshness. But the—um—general outlines are much as usual. In fact precisely as usual."

"Then that's all right." Wedge beamed again. "Even one's most reliable authors, you know, are liable to go right off the rails from time to time. Turn in something you'd never expect from them. Of course, it never does. Sells badly itself, and kills the succeeding book."

Petticate shook his head.

"I'm sure Sonia will never do anything like that. Certainly not if I have anything to do with it."

"That's fine. And you're tremendously useful to her, I know." In an access of what appeared to be sheer affection, Wedge fished a cigar box from a drawer and thrust it towards the husband of his esteemed authoress. "Havana," he said.

Petticate registered his gratified awareness of this impressive circumstance, and took a cigar.

"I've no doubt," he said, "that you have shocks from time to time."

"Lord, yes! Take Alspach. Your dear wife excepted"— and Wedge offered Petticate a frankly conspiratorial grin —"Alspach is quite the most distinguished writer on my list."

Petticate gave the sudden harsh cackle that commonly preluded his occasional assertion of those superior standards of judgment with which Providence had endowed him.

"Only one in your whole stable, my boy," he said.

"I wouldn't deny his being in a class by himself. In the running for an O.M., and so forth. You know his books. Always the same richly sombre tone. The still sad music of humanity. Deep sadness, majestic gravity, unfaltering compassion. That was Alspach—as solemn as Mrs. Humphry Ward, and a genius into the bargain. Then he had a spot of trouble at home."

"I'm sorry to hear it," Petticate offered conventionally.

"So, of course, was I." Wedge paused. "From a personal point of view, that is to say. Professionally regarded, it looked like being all to the good. His wife went mad. His only boy was killed while climbing in the Alps. They put his poor old father, who must have been over eighty, in jail. And then they told him that he himself was going incurably blind. Frankly, my dear chap, I expected by every post the Alspach that would put all previous Alspaches in the shade. The music stiller and sadder than ever, and everything else to match. Wasn't that reasonable?"

Petticate, although he was not very interested in Wedge's Alspach, gave this question decent consideration.

"Well, yes—unless the poor devil's misfortunes simply silenced him."

"They didn't. The manuscript came in, all right. But it was completely off the rails. Not Alspach at all. Sadness, gravity, compassion: he'd ditched the whole outfit. The book was a savage comedy, a diabolical farce. Did you ever hear anything as unaccountable as that?"

"Absolutely never." Petticate spoke promptly. It was not his part, he reflected, to argue with this useful imbecile—particularly as there might be tricky times ahead. He improved the occasion by asking: "May I tell Sonia about Alspach? She'll be terribly interested."

"Yes, of course. I wish she'd come up to town with you."

"Ah—that reminds me." Petticate appeared to hesitate. "Do you mind, my dear fellow, if I drop a word in your ear?"

Wedge looked momentarily suspicious.

"Go ahead," he said. "Go right ahead."

"It was nice of you to ask her to lunch today. But, between you and me, Sonia is just the tiniest bit touchy. Would you ask Alspach to lunch—provided he wasn't deprived and bereaved and blinded and turning in manuscripts filled with demoniacal laughter? What I mean to say is, it's perhaps time you did another of those rather grand dinners in Sonia's honour. A word to the wise, old boy."

"Thank you very much." Wedge appeared to take this hint in terms of sober gratitude. "I'll see what I can fix up."

"Only it will have to wait a bit, now. Sonia's off, you know. One of her wandering fits."

"I never heard that she had wandering fits." Wedge was interested. "Don't you usually take your holidays together —in the yacht, and so forth?"

"Yes, we do. But occasionally Sonia does just pack up

[17]

and clear out. A sort of restlessness. Time of life, I suppose. Sometimes I even feel she might do it in a big way."

"You don't mean leave you?" Wedge looked alarmed at these intimations of instability in Sonia Wayward.

"Not precisely that. Merely that the next thing one might hear of her could be a picture-postcard from Brazil. Fortunately it doesn't affect her output. Nothing affects that."

"Certainly nothing has ever affected it so far." Wedge remained slightly uneasy. "Does she take a secretary with her?"

"No, no. We're not made of gold, my dear fellow—even with your excellent conduct of our affairs. And Sonia's a great hand with a portable typewriter. Of course, when she's travelling, she sends everything to me to get copied and tidied up."

"You've been a very efficient agent of late." Wedge advanced this in a manner not wholly amiable.

"Well, there's no doubt that Sonia has come to like it that way. Receiving the money and keeping the accounts, and so forth. The job quite amuses me, you know, and it seems sensible enough. Business distracts her from her work. Cuts down output. The less it's obtruded on her, the better she gets along. Certainly, keeping her quite clear of it has worked well with this new book. I think I'm more interested in it than in anything else she's done."

Wedge was now wholly cheerful again.

"It builds up suspense?" he asked.

"Oh, most decidedly. I've been spending quite a lot of time wondering what's going to happen next."

For a moment Wedge appeared disposed to receive this

statement as a joke. Then he thought better of it.

"Fine," he said. He was disposed to affect faint Americanisms. "What's this one to be called?"

For a fraction of a second Petticate hesitated. It was, he believed, the first instance of his doing so since he had embarked—or it might be better to say disembarked—upon his deception. Did Sonia invariably fix on the title of a new book at the start, so that it was something Wedge took for granted? It just so happened that Petticate didn't know. So he must play safe.

"*The Gates of Delight*," he said. "She's going to call it *The Gates of Delight*. Rather good, I think. Discreetly erotic, but not vulgar." He gave his sudden cackle. "Or not at her level."

But Wedge was staring.

"*The Gates of Delight*? But that was the title of her—let me see—her third book! How can she possibly have forgotten?"

It was Petticate who had forgotten—or rather unconscious memory had neatly tripped him up.

"Yes, of course." He laughed easily, and was careful to be in no haste to retrieve his slip. Meanwhile he thought rapidly, and with the satisfactory result that the probable source of this long-past title of Sonia's came into his head. "I meant "*Man's Desire*," he said. "You can see how I mixed them up. That lovely ode by Bridges:

> *Open for me the gates of delight,*
> *The gates of the garden of man's desire;*
> *Where spirits touch'd by heavenly fire*
> *Have planted the trees of life.*

[19]

As a matter of fact, Sonia's thinking of taking a third title from the same stanza. *The Trees of Life*. I think I like that even better. But *The Gates of Delight*—I mean *Man's Desire*—is just the thing for what she's working at now."

Wedge was visibly impressed by this wealth of literary reference.

"*Man's Desire* isn't bad," he said. "Provided, naturally, it's the straight thing. We don't expect anything pathological from Sonia. The travellers wouldn't like it. And the reviewers mightn't either—although of course that's less important. Only one's travellers sell books. That, you know, is the great lesson we have to learn from the Yanks. In the field of literature, that is to say."

Petticate was silent for a moment. He was reflecting that hoodwinking such a donkey as Ambrose Wedge was really rather poor sport for a person as clever as himself.

"You'll find," he said, "that Sonia's new yarn, bless her, is as clean as a whistle. The Desire of Man is for the Woman, and the Desire of the Woman is for the Desire of the Man." Petticate cackled. "Such profundities reach the circulating libraries pretty rapidly, these days. The suburbs march breast forwards with Maugham. And Sonia keeps up. And she'll keep on keeping up, if you ask me."

"Alive," Wedge said.

"Just that." Petticate accepted the word with enthusiasm. "Unquenchable vitality. I'm pretty sure Sonia will be going strong for as long as I live."

"Nice for you." Wedge, perhaps faintly aware that he was in some fashion being mocked at, made one of his detours into the disagreeable. "Keeps the wolf from the door, doesn't it? Or even right at the bottom of the garden."

Petticate laughed what was by this time his deft liar's laugh.

"I have my modest private competence, you know, as well as my absurd pittance of a pension from the army. But naturally it's delightful that the world treats Sonia so well. Last year was a pretty good one, I think you'll agree."

"It wasn't at all bad. In fact the sales were excellent." Wedge spoke as a fair-minded man. "Only they cost us something, I don't mind telling you. It was quite a battle on the promotion side."

"Was it, indeed?" Petticate sounded discreetly sceptical. "I don't remember noticing that your advertising was anything out of the way."

"Advertising?" Wedge, although he had now assumed the appearance of one sunk under a weight of care, managed an indulgent smile. "My dear chap, you don't think advertisements sell books nowadays? It's having the crack team of travellers that does the trick, every time. Unfortunately they're devilishly expensive. I'd like to have you meet them, some time. They're an—um—fine body of men." Wedge paused. "And women," he added as an afterthought. "I must certainly have you meet them one day."

Petticate, who had no belief in the substantial existence of this *régiment d'élite*, allowed himself a moment's unresponsive silence.

"I should mention," he said presently, "that I've been having a certain amount of business talk with Sonia—before she went off, that is. She started it, surprisingly enough. I'd say the royalty rates are a bit on her mind. Of course I tell her not to worry, and that I'll look after all that. That's much the best thing, you'll agree."

Wedge considered this.

"It has," he said rather ambiguously, "its advantages, no doubt."

"I've been thinking about that sliding scale. Quite frankly, I'd like to see the twenty per cent begin to operate a good deal earlier."

Wedge gave the sort of brisk nod that characterises a man of eminently open mind.

"My dear fellow, I'll try to meet you if I possibly can. Only do remember"—Wedge produced a charmingly frank smile, and at the same time achieved a practiced gesture, sweeping in the threadbare drugget and horsehair upholsteries of the deceased solicitor—"only do remember that, in this trade, one lives positively from five-pound note to five-pound note."

Petticate looked at his cigar—not so much by way of un-generous comment upon Wedge's last remark as in calcula-tion of how much longer he might spend where he was. It had occurred to him that, given a little ingenuity, Wedge could be made to work for a few of those five-pound notes.

"Am I right," he asked, "in seeming to remember that those travellers of yours like to take round a sort of trailer of the next book?"

"Certainly. And Sonia usually manages to let me have something when she's about halfway through." Wedge tapped his own cigar against an ash-tray thoughtfuly do-nated to his impoverished enterprise by a firm of mineral-water manufacturers. "Do you think that, when you get in touch with her, you could ask her to send something of the sort along?"

"I certainly can—if I *do* get in touch with her. But it's

my guess that I shan't have a word from her until *Man's Desire* is finished. Of course, I have a carbon of those first thirty thousand words. So I could probably knock you up something myself. I told you—didn't I?—that I find it a deuced interesting story. As a matter of fact, most of what I've read is quite vividly in my head."

"How very odd." Wedge frowned, as if at once disapproving his own rash dip into candour. "Does it begin in an artist's studio, or abroad the *Queen Mary*, or just before Lord Somebody's guests start to arrive for a house party?"

"It begins in an artist's studio. An elderly and eminent sculptor called Paul Vedrenne. An Englishman, of course."

Wedge nodded.

"But of an old Huguenot family?"

"Certainly. And he has a son called Timmy, who isn't an artist, but who gives his father a hand with the roughwork from time to time. Slogging away at the marble, you know, in the early stages of some colossal design. Timmy isn't happy—I'll explain about that in a moment—and this making the chips fly affords him a certain amount of relief from nervous tension. He's occupied in this way when the girl calls."

"Corn-coloured hair?" Wedge asked. "Or dusky and smouldering?"

"Honey-coloured. She has great honey-coloured ramparts at her ears."

"Good Lord!" Wedge was respectful. "How does Sonia think of these things? It's positively poetical—that about the ramparts."

Petticate cackled.

"It ought to be, my dear chap, since it's stolen from Yeats. This girl, who's called Claire . . ."

Wedge shook his head doubtfully.

"Aren't Claires out?"

"Her name can be changed if necessary. Her father is a great industrialist. But she's a nice girl, because her mother's people have lived in Shropshire for quite a long time. And —as I say—she calls at Paul Vedrenne's studio, with a message about a bust that Vedrenne has been commissioned to do of her affluent father. And there is Timmy Vedrenne, chipping away like mad. He is stripped to the buff."

"To the what?"

"The buff. Better than to the waist, because more indefinite. Means simply to the skin."

Wedge looked alarmed.

"Oh, I say—that won't do at all! Dash it, he must wear something."

Petticate waved a reassuring hand.

"That's all right. The buff is modified to the extent of an old pair of rowing shorts. Timmy Vedrenne has rowed for Oxford."

"At stroke—and faster than all the rest?" Wedge appeared delighted at the aptness with which he had resuscitated this ancient joke at the expense of the female fiction. "Tell Sonia that rowing shorts are most uncomfortable to stand up in. They're tailored to the male figure when crouched over a bloody oar. Don't I remember it."

"No doubt." Petticate allowed no pause in which Wedge could enlarge on his own athletic past. "But there the lad is—and there's an uncommonly good description of him in action."

"Golden torso, ripple of muscle under the fine skin, loins of darkness, and all that?"

"Not *of darkness*, my dear chap. Dash it all, Sonia has

some taste in the way in which her work shows—um—literary derivations. She doesn't set Lawrence and all those fellows absolutely screaming at you. Just *loins*. Perhaps slim loins in one place. Anyway, Timmy is a nice boy. So Claire is terribly upset later on, when she discovers him in bed with her horrible baby-snatching Aunt Sophia."

"A sister of the affluent industrialist?"

"Of course. Claire's aunts on her mother's side are so aristocratic that they regard sex as interesting only when it happens among dogs or horses. Naturally, Claire's discovery is delicately done. She doesn't grossly gape on the thing, as Iago says. It's those rowing shorts. Timmy has brought them to a house party, where there's to be a certain amount of fun on the river. And Claire sees them draped over the balcony of Aunt Sophia's bedroom. Poor girl—they are engraved upon her mind, and she would know them anywhere. But she's a girl of spirit. She climbs up to that balcony, and slips into a pocket of the shorts—"

"Rowing shorts don't have pockets."

"Nowadays they do—or, if they don't, the readers will never notice it. Because the moment's a very moving one. Claire slips into that pocket a flower that Timmy had plucked for her in the garden the evening before."

"Bad form for guests to pluck flowers."

"Timmy isn't exactly a guest. The place belongs to his godfather, who is a peer and a Cabinet Minister. The Vedrennes have kept on being well connected ever since they slipped out of the Massacre of St Bartholomew, or whatever it was. Anyway, Timmy finds the flower—crumpled and faded, which makes the symbolism of the thing uncommonly elegant, you'll agree. So he knows that he's been found out. And he's more unhappy than ever. You can see

[25]

it in his eyes. They're inscrutable and inchoate. And that's as far as the thing goes."

"Leaving you," Wedge asked, "dead keen to know how it will go on?"

"Certainly—as all Sonia's readers will be." Petticate paused. "What's *your* guess," he asked, "about what happens next?"

Wedge waved his cigar airily. He appeared amused by Petticate's question.

"My dear fellow," he asked, "is it really a matter of guess-work? Isn't it rather a matter of inference? But I don't think I have all the facts. Is Claire's Aunt Sophia a married woman?"

Petticate thought for a moment.

"Yes," he said. "She is. Her husband's pretty dim, as Sonia rates them—merely a top-ranking surgeon, or something of the sort—but he's there."

"And this fellow Timmy Vedrenne is to get Claire in the end? A wedding at St. Margaret's, and all that?"

"That's just what I'm asking you. But I'd suppose so. As I've said, it's Sonia's usual charming thing, and one can't doubt that sunshine will bathe the last pages. You wouldn't have her taking over from Alspach, would you?"

Wedge answered this only with a gesture of horrified repudiation.

"Very well," he said. "If the story's to be kept from going badly off the rails, one thing is clear. Timmy wasn't sleeping with Aunt Sophia, after all. You can involve your hero in a little fornication, you know, provided he goes about it in a good-hearted sort of way. But adultery is out. In no wholesome and popular fiction does an adulterer finally marry the heroine. Take Shakespeare."

"And what the devil has Shakespeare to do with it?" The cultivated soul of Colonel Petticate was outraged that a name of some distinction in the chronicles of authentic art should thus be cited by the ludicrous Wedge. "Aren't we talking about the plumbing?"

Wedge, fortunately, was too taken up in his subject to notice this oddly savage *volte face* on the part of the admiring husband of Sonia Wayward. He pursued his theme.

"In all Shakespeare's plays, my boy, it happens only once. And that's in the very special case of What's-his-name, whom they'd bullied into marrying the lady doctor."

"Bertram and Helena," Petticate said coldly. "But I suppose you're right. If Timmy has slept with Sophia, then repentance in Claire's arms—which is the honest, real-life thing—won't do within the conventions of Sonia's curious world. Do you know, it hadn't struck me? And yet I felt I knew Sonia's vein of romance quite well." And Petticate stared rather thoughtfully at the diminishing length of his cigar.

"You haven't considered it analytically," Wedge said, and shook his head with an air of high intelligence. "You'll find that what Sonia does about those rowing shorts on Aunt Sophia's balcony is simply to explain them away." This time Wedge nodded weightily. "That's it. She'll simply explain them away."

"But you forget that the boy has been terribly unhappy all the time. We first met him like that, when he was taking it out of his eminent father's best-quality marble. And that can only be because he had some sense of guilt."

"My dear chap, that's something utterly different." Wedge spoke with fine assurance. "It's something that shows he has quite exceptionally fine feelings. He failed, I'd say, to visit his old nanny on her deathbed. It was a real fault. But the dear fellow has got it all out of proportion, and Claire is eventually going to give him a sane view of the matter. Mark my word—she'll confess some similar mild turpitude from her own childhood days. I'll wager you a dozen of champagne on it." Wedge seemed to recall that he was one whom the service of literature kept on the near fringes of destitution. "That is," he emended, "a dozen of drinkable Beaujolais."

Petticate was impressed—and not least by his own address in thus eliciting some useful information about hitherto unsuspected pitfalls in the production of popular fiction.

"I've no doubt," he said, "that Sonia's mind is working precisely as you say. But I'll be uncommonly interested to discover how she gets round that pair of pants."

"What they call an artificial plot, my boy. Perhaps a spot of calumny. In romance, you'll find, balconies have always been great places for nasty machinations of that sort. Think of that other wench in Shakespeare—the one that gets called a rotten orange."

"Hero," Petticate said with renewed chilliness.

"That's right. Dumb sort of kid. They made out she was entertaining a lover. Wonderful expression that, isn't it? Well, perhaps there's somebody in Sonia's book who's just making out that Aunt Sophia has been entertaining Timmy." Wedge chuckled. "Torso and all," he added.

Petticate frowned. He always deprecated coarse talk.

"It's a possibility," he said.

"Or Aunt Sophia may a little dote on the young man in a respectably motherly way. She may have found the shorts down by the river, and decided to wash them for the dear lad, and then hung them out to dry on her balcony. Only it wouldn't be easy to give much dramatic colouring to a mere misunderstanding like that. I come back to deliberate deception by some jealous and malign person as much the likeliest thing."

"I think you'll prove to be right." Unconsciously, Petticate spoke as one who weighs his words and arrives at a decision of moment. "And I've no doubt that you can rely upon the delivery of the manuscript pretty soon."

"Even with things as they are?"

Petticate was to wonder whether this question had left him for a fraction of a second just discernibly blank. But memory quickly returned to him and he replied easily enough.

"Oh, dear me, yes. I thought I'd made that clear. Sonia's going wandering won't affect the matter in the slightest. And as for the story, what may appear difficulties to us will be plain sailing to her."

"A lucid mind," Wedge said contentedly. "Bright and clear and sparkling—although not, between you and me, precisely given to sounding the depths."

"Certainly not that." Petticate, finding his cigar finished, had got to his feet. "I don't remember," he said as he shook hands with Wedge, "Sonia's ever getting into deep water."

3

It was in a reasonably contented frame of mind that Colonel Ffolliot Petticate settled himself into a first-class compartment of the 4:45 from Paddington. As he walked past the second-class coaches—cluttered with string-bags and brown-paper parcels, sticky with children, and generally given over to the horrors of plebeian life—they had struck him as a vivid illustration of the penury which his resolute conduct during the past forty-eight hours had put him fairly in the way of escaping. Widows in reduced circumstances are a dismal lumber enough; a widower in similar straits must necessarily be not only dismal but ridiculous as well. To sit in the pit and to be there remarked by old companions of the stalls; to drive up in some clever little foreign car to the houses of friends whom one has hitherto visited in a respectable English sedan; to have to think twice about a new suit, or even about picking up half a dozen ties in the Burlington Arcade; to slip warily into the shops of licenced grocers for the purpose of buying colonial sherry: Colonel Petticate could visualise only too vividly a sort of intensifying series of such encounters with darkness. He was not a spendthrift, and the breadth of his intellectual and aesthetic interests had the natural consequence of rendering him largely superior to sordid material consideration of any sort. Still, there were limits. And fortune, he knew, would have been ready to cast him remorselessly beyond the pale, had he not risen up before his unlooked-for crisis and declared himself to be the master of his own fate and the captain—indeed the colonel—of his own soul.

And so far, he told himself, so good. It had been admirable strategy to tackle Wedge straight away. Wedge was cast for the role of his principal dupe—if "dupe," indeed, was not a word exceptionable as carrying inappropriate suggestions of fraud. Perhaps "unconscious collaborator" would be better. Petticate registered a faint grin as he made this silent correction in his own thought. He was really in excellent spirits.

Wedge had eaten out of his hand. And this desirable state of affairs he had brought off almost without a thought. His own temerity almost scared him in the retrospect—although it gratified him, too. For he had simply walked in and extemporized. It was only his grand design—only the broadest outline of the beckoning glimmering thing—that had been in the least clear to him. Even now, when he had spent, before catching the train, a meditative hour in his club, he had done nothing to fill in the picture. Just in what circumstances had his wife parted from him? He had no idea. Had she intimated any proposed destination—and, if so, what? He had no idea of this either. To Wedge he had murmured something about Brazil, but that had been by way of more or less airy hypothesis. If Wedge had been more curious, had asked even two or three searching questions, his own trust in the inspiration of the moment might conceivably have failed him. So he must really go about the matter more systematically. Nearly the whole of the spadework, he could see, was yet to do.

Not, fortunately, that Sonia had made any call upon spadework in the literal sense. The happy circumstances of her decease had obviated the need for any arduous toil at the bottom of that garden from which the dear old girl's labours had—in Wedge's rather impertinent image—hitherto excluded the wolf.

This start of graveyard wit so amused Petticate that he almost laughed aloud. But to have done so, he suddenly realised, would have been unfortunate, since the compartment now held another passenger. Nor—and he had been most remiss in not remarking this earlier—was this second passenger a stranger. He was, in fact, old Dr. Gregory, Petticate's physician and near neighbour. And Dr. Gregory, observing that he had been observed, now spoke.

"Afternoon, Petticate. Another of those heavy lunches, eh?"

Petticate made what reply he considered judicious to this unceremonious greeting. Although his mental state was now so satisfactory, it was conceivable, he realised, that he was looking physically a little off-colour. He had had a nasty shock, after all. But, of course, he couldn't tell old Gregory about *that*. Indeed, he couldn't safely tell him anything at all, since Gregory represented his first contact with the rural society amid which he lived, and whatever story was to be circulated through that society must be meditated with care. No more happy extemporization. The thing must be thought out in all its bearings. *Now*. Before this journey was over.

Petticate, having thus determined, offered a single further civil remark to Dr. Gregory, and then unfolded his *Times* —that ritual gesture whereby an English gentleman claims inviolable privacy for a season. Dr. Gregory in his turn opened *The British Medical Journal*. The train was not due out for another ten minutes. Petticate turned to the page which Printing House Square dedicates weekly to the interests of female readers. This was not the consequence of a nostalgic thought for Sonia. He judged it the page least likely to distract his thoughts from the important task before them.

Dispassionately put, his project involved two kinds—and, he supposed, degrees—of forgery. There was forgery as it had been pursued by James Macpherson in the laudible interest of endowing the world with an ancient Gaelic epic, or by William Ireland in the yet more commendable endeavour to add to the number of surviving plays by Shakespeare. Petticate was not very clear about the legal aspect of this part of his plans. Plenty of books published as being by X were in fact in whole or part the work of Y. But there was no doubt a point at which this sort of thing might elicit the disapprobation of the Law Officers of the Crown—and if they couldn't get at you one way, it was pretty certain that they could get at you another.

Income tax, for instance. There was certainly a field to which he would have to give most careful consideration. It would be foolish to deny that very considerable hazards awaited him. Some of them he was, no doubt, still in no position to take account of. They would bob up unexpectedly as a ready test of wit. He hadn't, for instance, until that talk with Wedge, quite succeeded in getting into clear focus the business of the morality of popular fiction. Still, he had hold of that now, and he would write nothing to shock the sensibilities of those wives of the clergy who no doubt formed a solid block of Sonia's readers.

That sort of forgery was going to be plain sailing. The more technical kind—that involving the actual simulating of Sonia's signature—was really going to crop up surprisingly seldom. When a new agreement had to be made with publishers, the signature must appear on it. But such an agreement would always contain—as for some years it had contained—a clause requiring all payments to be made to the author's agent, Colonel Petticate, whose discharge thereof would be final. That was, in the world of publishing, common form. And it meant that once the money was in Colonel Petticate's bank, its further destination was nobody's business but his own—his own and that of a nonexistent lady. There was perhaps no other profession or occupation in the world, Petticate happily speculated, to the pursuit of which mere continued fleshly existence was so inessential.

Of course there was a natural term to the thing. He could scarcely hope to pursue his new activity beyond his own ninetieth birthday, since by that date Sonia Wayward would be verifiable from *Who's Who* as well over a hundred, and not very plausibly, therefore, to be represented as still in the full vigour of her career. Still, there was plenty of scope between now and then.

Petticate chuckled—but without eliciting any surprise from Dr. Gregory, who naturally supposed his diversion to be occasioned by one of the *Time's* irresistably humorous Fourth Leaders.

Income tax. There was really no difficulty there either. Every year Sonia must sign a return of income—and perhaps a receipt or two if the Commissioners generously decided, as they sometimes do, to send some inconsiderable

[34]

trifle back. But nobody is going to scrutinize that sort of signature. Of course any sort of trouble over taxation would be fatal, and he would now himself have to do all the accounting with a care that should insure that no awkward inquiries were ever launched. Sonia's own bank account presented another problem. There would have to be a letter closing that—and it is precisely to a banker that one doesn't care to send a signature which is not quite all it should be. Still, there was only a minor risk there. In fact it looked as if, on the business and legal side, common prudence would again insure sailing that was plain enough. It was in the social sphere that the real conundrums lay.

He must decide, in the first place, where Sonia had gone to. It was all very well being airy with Wedge, but with his neighbours at Snigg's Green another and different technique would be required. To announce that his wife had departed into the blue would be to invite no end of gossip. On the other hand, if he acquiesced in the natural assumption that he knew her whereabouts, there would presently be requests for her address from people who wanted to correspond with her on one trifling occasion or another. So Sonia must be represented as having gone away in circumstances that precluded her having a known address for the time being, but which held out the expectation of her being heard from quite soon. That would afford a breathing space. And during that breathing space he must decide what he himself was going to do.

He had, he told himself, great freedom of manoeuvre. A successful novelist can take up residence pretty well in any corner of the globe that strikes her fancy—and so can her husband, if he happens to be a retired professional man of independent means. Taxation and the servant problem being what they were, people in their position were constantly going off nowadays to settle in quarters which would have been regarded as merely outlandish a generation ago. Sonia, in fact, had only to find some enchanting spot to which she should summon him in her well-known imperious way. And he had only to pack his trunks and follow her.

The whole thing must be made not too vague and yet not too precise. It wouldn't do, for instance, to name Nassau or Nairobi, since that might well lead to pilgrims from Snigg's Green or elsewhere making casual attempt to look them up. "Sonia has almost settled on the Bahamas, but the Bermudas are another possibility." Something like that must be the formula. And once he himself had got plausibly away under cover of it, almost nothing could go wrong.

Apart from a vague cloud of distant cousins, Sonia had no surviving relations. He himself, although possessed, of course, of a certain inherent distinction, had long been content with a private station in virtue of which the world was likely to take very little interest in his movements or circumstances. If permanent exile didn't suit him, and he much doubted whether it would, he could always come home for a month of two now and then, explaining to anybody who enquired that his wife's health—or perhaps just her unremitting devotion to the art of fiction—did not admit of her travelling at the moment. He might even, if he thought out the problems clearly beforehand, revisit Snigg's Green and treat its inhabitants to a great deal of agreeable fantasy. For there was no doubt—Petticate told himself, still behind his *Times*—that he would come to take a virtuoso's delight in the whole delicious deception. That he would be fooling people on rather a large scale—for, after all, didn't tens

[36]

of thousands of people regularly look out for the new Sonia Wayward?—was the particular charm of the whole situation.

Colonel Petticate had reached this entirely satisfactory point in his reflections, and had become aware, from without, of the slightly enhanced bustle that preluded his departure for the next stage of his adventure, when the voice of Dr. Gregory sounded from across the compartment.

"Petticate," Dr. Gregory said, "doesn't it look as if your wife is going to miss the train?"

4

It was the first unexpected question he had been asked about Sonia. And he didn't stand up to it at all well. In fact he lowered his newspaper and stared at Dr. Gregory in consternation.

"My wife!" he said.

There was a moment's silence in which he realised that he spoken the word rather wildly—so that it would scarcely have surprised him to hear himself add, like the unfortunate Moor of Venice, *What wife? I have no wife*. Quite abruptly, he had almost met absolute shipwreck.

And Dr. Gregory was giving him a sharp look.

"I ran across her at the bookstall," he said.

"Sonia?" Petticate was entirely surprised to hear his own voice. He had very strongly the sensation—sometimes referred to in Sonia's fictions—of being struck dumb. "You spoke to her?"

"No, no—I merely noticed her buying a magazine." Dr. Gregory paused as the guard's whistle blew. "She *has* missed it," he added.

It ought certainly to have been true. Only it wasn't. For, even as Dr. Gregory spoke, there was a shout on the platform, a door opened and then banged shut again—and Petticate, glancing, already pale and stricken, into the corridor, saw with frozen horror his wife standing there. It was only for a second's space. She had boarded, along with a suitcase, the already moving train. And then instantly she had vanished in search of another compartment.

Dr. Gregory had seen nothing of this preternatural catastrophe. He had been much too occupied in staring at Petticate, towards whom he now leant forward for the purpose of making a professional grab at his wrist.

"Keep still," Dr. Gregory said. "Breathe easily. And don't be alarmed. Just a digestive matter. It will pass off in a few minutes." He accompanied these remarks with a glance in which Petticate, even in his prostration, recognised the plainest expectation of immediate fatality. No doubt Gregory supposed him to have suffered a severe cerebral thrombosis.

The perception of this hopelessly erroneous diagnosis almost steadied Petticate. Gregory had always been a bit of an ass.

"You're quite right," he heard himself say. "Flatulence, Gregory—just a touch of flatulence. Been troubled a little by it lately. And you needn't bother about that pulse."

Gregory sat back. In appearance, at least, Petticate must have rallied. Nevertheless his mind was in a dreadful state. It was not the less so because it had registered, at least for a brief moment, enormous relief. Sonia was alive! The thing hadn't happened. It had been all a dream.

Petticate closed his eyes, and tried to accept Dr. Gregory's advice to breathe easily. He searched for proofs and signs—for anything in his recent circumstances that would render indubitable the fact that it *had* been a dream; that he had suffered a terrible nightmare in which he had appeared to lose his wife. But he searched, of course, in vain. He hadn't just woken up. He *had* lost Sonia. He *had* himself done that thing. . . .

And yet she was on board the train. Sonia—or was it Sonia's ghost?—was within a few yards of him now. Still with his eyes closed, Petticate set his mind painfully to work. Not a ghost—because there is no such thing. And not a hallucination. He could give himself no reason for knowing this, but he did know it, all the same. There had been real flesh and blood in the corridor. It was the real Sonia. She was on her way home.

But it was impossible, he told himself. And then, in an instantaneous flash that brought simultaneously a rush of horror and of relief, he saw the entirely naturalistic, the perfectly rational truth of the matter. The Sonia who had seemed to sink for ever beneath the waters of the English Channel had been not dead but alive. He had been too cocksure, too confident of his sadly rusty medical expertness. Almost, he had been aware of that at the time. And now real professional knowledge came back to him. He remembered cases of trance, of suddenly induced coma, of which he had read. When that sort of thing happened— and it *did* happen, although admittedly it was rare—only tests far more searching than he had applied could distinguish between the resulting suspended animation and actual death. That was it!

But, even so . . . ? And then he recalled the other yacht. He had been very shaky, and the sight of that unexpected yacht so close at hand had pretty well finished him for the time. He had staggered into the cabin, and anything might have happened after that. Probably the shock of her sudden immersion had brought Sonia back to consciousness. And, knowing what he had done, she had managed to attract the attention of that other craft, and had been taken on board it. Then she had persuaded its owners to sail straight on. She had done that because she was already nursing some diabolical scheme of revenge.

The sudden glimpse of this extreme wickedness in Sonia upset Petticate even more violently than the first shock of her return had done. From head to foot, he suddenly discovered himself to be bathed in an icy sweat. And Gregory was looking at him in that queer way again. He found he couldn't stand it. He staggered to his feet.

"Just going along the corridor," he muttered almost incoherently. And then he escaped from the compartment.

Petticate stumbled down the corridor with his senses in considerable disorder. Far on his left hand, he was perfectly aware of the silhouette of Windsor Castle against the skyline. But on the persons seated immediately behind the plate glass on his right, his vision refused to give him any intelligible report. He was clearly too apprehensive of what he might glimpse there. Probably he had been rash to emerge from his own compartment. If Sonia saw him— as, almost certainly, she had not done when she tumbled into the train—it might precipitate a crisis. It might bring about at once an appalling public exposure, which otherwise he might yet find some means of avoiding. His best plan would be to lock himself into the nearest lavatory and *think*.

Petticate did this. It was a resource altogether distasteful to his refined sensibilities, the more so when people came and rattled at the door. Such behaviour in first-class passengers, if they *were* first-class passengers, struck him as unseemly if not positively immoral. He stood by the window and peered through the little oval of clear glass, set high in the pane, which was all that the modesty of this apartment permitted by way of glimpse of the outer world.

He had better, he thought, murder Sonia.

The abrupt emergence of this idea occasioned Petticate great dismay. Here was the logical course to pursue—and yet only a few minutes ago the emotion which knowledge of his wife's continued existence prompted in him had been one of vast relief! It was evident that he was in some state of intellectual confusion. There was, of course, nothing that he more disliked. He had better forget about that feeling of relief—which had demonstrably proceeded from some muddle unworthy of him—and get to work upon the details of his new and entirely rational proposal. For there could be no doubt as to the necessity of the thing. Sonia's present conduct was incompatible with anything other than some plan for his utter exposure and confusion.

He had no time, in fact, to spare. And there was just a possibility, he thought, that Sonia, who like himself would be travelling first-class, might be discovered in a compartment by herself. Perhaps, having located her, he could simply rush in, hurl open the door at the farther end of the compartment, and pitch her through it? *That* would almost certainly do the trick, since they must be travelling at over sixty miles an hour.

It was an excellent plan, because an utterly simple one. Then he realised, with a shock of dismay, that it had been conceived by a mind fatally behind the times. Railway coaches such as these no longer *had* doors at the farther side; their only mode of egress was through the corridor. And unless, as was most unlikely, Sonia had a whole coach to herself, bundling her first into the corridor and then through another door on to the permanent way would simply not be feasible.

Petticate sat down—it was again a disagreeable thing to do—and reviewed other methods of killing a vigorous woman in early middle age. The one course he must avoid, and he saw this with perfect clarity, was that of relying upon any of those methods which were peculiarly within the scope of his own profession. It must not—decidedly it must not—be anything that could be called a doctor's murder.

Surprisingly in one whose mental processes were normally so acute, Colonel Petticate spent a good fifteen minutes in these lethal reveries. In fact the train was already running into Reading before it dawned on him that all these drastic thoughts were needless. Why ever should he murder poor old Sonia? Surely all that was necessary was to insist that she was off her head? For he had himself, so far, said and done nothing at all which could be taken to bear out the unlikely story she would have to tell.

It was true that he had arrived back in port without her and said nothing. But if she had been, say, in some state of evident emotional disturbance, and had insisted on being somewhere set quietly ashore, his subsequent conduct could only be read as having been thoroughly discreet. Of course there would be difficulties. It was going to be embarrassing to have Sonia running round with such an extraordinary yarn. And if she persisted in it, and he found it necessary to have the poor soul confined in a mental hospital, it would scarcely be possible to carry out his engaging plan of writing all the new Sonia Waywards himself. If, on the other hand, Sonia thought better of her plan of public denunciation, it was unlikely that she would be willing to have much to do with him in future—or even to support him in the station of life to which he was accustomed.

So perhaps, after all, and despite the fact that there could be no legal case against him, he had better proceed as planned. A fire? A car accident? He could not be certain that Sonia had not already told her story to someone. It was a possibility that made his task a peculiarly delicate one.

The people on that yacht. Suddenly, and with a fresh chill of dismay, Petticate realised that he had been leaving them fatally out of account. Whatever story *he* told must be made to square with the fact that they had veritably fished Sonia out of the sea. And this, when he came to ponder it, just couldn't be done. Accident might have taken Sonia overboard. Or she might have jumped into the sea as a first expression of the lunacy which subsequently prompted her to a baseless charge against her husband. But nothing could account for that husband's keeping quiet about it and giving out that his wife had simply departed on some sort of holiday. Nothing whatever.

Petticate saw that he had now at last accurately analysed the whole situation. And he just didn't know where to turn. In fact, it wasn't Sonia Wayward who was at sea, after all. It was her husband. Murder wouldn't do—for as soon as the people in the yacht told their story he would almost certainly be done for. Only one course remained open to him: the most disagreeable he could conceive. He must throw himself on Sonia's mercy.

[44]

After all, he said to himself as he unlocked the lavatory door and emerged again into the corridor, it wasn't as if he had acted in any criminal way against Sonia. On the contrary, hadn't he just this moment turned down the idea of murdering her? He had never even acted in any unfriendly spirit against her. If he had been a trifle unceremonious with her, that had been when he had supposed her to be dead. What he had done had been the result partly of shock and partly of a positively laudable plan to keep, so to speak, Sonia Wayward's flag flying. If Sonia were reasonable—but unfortunately no woman is that—she would feel, on balance, that she owed him a certain gratitude for his conduct of the affair.

Of course she might be nursing entirely mistaken notions. She might imagine that it *hadn't* been a mere dead body that he had supposed himself to have chucked overboard. If this were so, the sooner he made an effort to re-establish himself in her good graces the better. It would be very awkward, for instance, if unjust indignation, bubbling up in her during the course of this journey, prompted her to leave the train at Oxford—which was the next stop —for the purpose of communicating with the police. Yes, he had better nerve himself to seek her out at once. There was something to be said, perhaps, for a first interview in the publicity, or semi-publicity, of a railway compartment.

Petticate moved forward along the train. His vision was at least no longer playing tricks with him, and he could take in his fellow travellers, compartment by compartment, as he walked. There wasn't, after all, any great crowd. Here and there even a second-class compartment was entirely empty. In others there were pieces of hand luggage but no passengers. That meant that people were having tea in the restaurant-car in front. Perhaps Sonia was there.

He went on, glancing into one compartment after another. It was a most disagreeable occupation. At any moment he might find himself looking into the accusing eyes of his wife. The thought made him remember—and for a second or two it brought a quite fresh sense of shock—that they were eyes which he had clumsily attempted to close, when Sonia was lying in her coma in the cockpit of the yacht. Her eyes, being a very unusual dark green, were her most striking feature. And Petticate felt a most disconcerting dread at the prospect of meeting them. Nevertheless he pressed on. He pressed on, in fact, until he was brought up short by colliding with some massive but more or less pneumatic obstacle. He had been so intent upon the successive compartments as he passed them that he had bumped straight into a passenger walking in the other direction.

Much to Petticate's alarm, the passenger roared aloud. And he was very little reassured when he realised that the roar was a roar of laughter, and moreover that it proceeded through female lips. There could be only one explanation, and a glance, as he recovered balance, assured him of its correctness. Here, most disastrously, was another neighbour. It was Mrs. Gotlop herself.

"Why—if it isn't my own enchanting Blimp!"

Mrs. Gotlop, who combined large expanses of tweed with a profusion of rings, earrings and bangles of obtrusively barbaric suggestion, had seized Petticate's hand in a savage grip. He disliked this even more than being greeted with such a foolish and impertinent nickname. But no sort of indignation ever registered with Mrs. Gotlop, and by now Petticate was, after all, pretty well used to her. For Augusta Gotlop did not merely live at Snigg's Green. She was an authoress of talent, and as such at once the rival and the familiar of Sonia Wayward.

"Ruddy Blimp!" Mrs. Gotlop shouted this not so much, it seemed, by way of further jovial insult as in tribute to Petticate's complexion, which still presumably bore, despite the ghastly pallors to which it had of late been intermittently reduced, the tokens of his recent marine vacation. "And rural Blimp! And martial Blimp!" Mrs. Gotlop robustly continued, still straightforwardly torturing Petticate's right hand. "What a sight for sore eyes, after all those bloodless bookworms in the British Museum!"

Petticate managed to murmur an expression of hope that Mrs. Gotlop's researches in the reading room of the Museum were approaching their usual successful termination. Mrs. Gotlop's books were always biographies of minor eighteenth-century notabilities, and what her scholarly investigations invariably brought for the first time to the light of day were episodes of blameless sentiment which blended admirably with Mrs. Gotlop's sweet and faded prose. For Mrs. Gotlop was a striking instance of the disparity which often exists between a writer when commanded by his or her Muse, and the same writer when going about his or her common diurnal occasions. Whereas Sonia Wayward was exactly like *her* books, Augusta Gotlop was precisely *not*. Petticate felt that he preferred Sonia. Indeed, swaying in the corridor of this horrible train, and gripped still in the paw of this appalling woman, he felt a sudden strong nostalgic affection for Sonia, so that he positively longed to locate her. It was this feeling that controlled his next utterance.

"You don't happen to have seen Sonia, by any chance?"

"Here on the train? Not a sliver of the darling!" Mrs. Gotlop laughed loudly, unnervingly, but apparently for mere laughter's sake. "Why, you haven't lost her, have you?"

"No, no. That's to say, I rather think she just caught the train. Perhaps she's having tea. I'm going forward to look." Petticate was confused. He had a notion that he mustn't say anything that was inconsistent with whatever he had said to old Dr. Gregory. But he couldn't remember whether, to old Dr. Gregory, he had said anything relevant at all. Nor, just for a second, could he remember just what he was really on his way to do. There had been something about throwing Sonia out of the train. Was that it? But, no—of course it wasn't. He had seen that for some reason action of that sort was no good. Reconciliation— that was what was on the carpet.

Petticate, startled to find his wits working so badly, now made some effort simply to push past Mrs. Gotlop. But she was a large woman, and here in the narrow corridor the operation involved an awkward and even indelicate squeeze. It was at the crisis of this, and when his face was within a couple of inches of hers, that Mrs. Gotlop started shouting again.

"Drinks!" Mrs. Gotlop shouted. "Drinks! Drinks!"

Petticate understood that this was an invitation, and one which certainly included Sonia as well as himself.

"That would be delightful," he muttered—muttered because he found it difficult to talk virtually straight into Mrs. Gotlop's teeth. "Some time."

"No, no! Tomorrow! Drinks! Usual time!" Mrs. Gotlop's laughter gained a new resonance. "If Sonia doesn't mind meeting her rascal of a publisher."

"Wedge?" This time, Petticate didn't mutter. He gasped.

"Certainly, certainly! Ambrose Wedge is to be week-ending with the Shotovers at Little Stoat. And Rickie Shotover has promised to bring him over. Gin galore!"

Petticate's disgust of a woman who could say "Gin ga-lore" was quite swallowed up in vexation. Even if he could square Sonia so that they told a common story, it would be extremely awkward if Wedge and Mrs. Gotlop exchanged notes. And, of course, they were sure to. It would emerge that he had told Wedge that Sonia had gone off into the blue, and had assured Mrs. Gotlop, only a few hours later, that they were travelling home together on the same train. It didn't matter very much, perhaps. With Sonia alive after all, what might crudely be called exposure carried hazards less dire than they would other-wise have been. But Petticate liked neatness in everything round about him. And the Sonia business had become, to say the least, quite desperately untidy.

"Thank you very much," he said, as he finally negoti-ated Mrs. Gotlop's right hip. "I'll have to see how I'm fixed." He frowned, conscious that there was something slightly ominous in this precise turn of phrase. And then he added with deliberate bravado: "Sonia, you know. I can't be sure what she may be cooking up for me over the next few days. Good-bye."

And Petticate fled down the corridor.

He had gone quite a long way, and was supposing that there could be only one or two more coaches before the restaurant-car, when his attention was caught and held, quite unaccountably, by an empty second-class compartment. Not indeed that it was quite empty. There was a suitcase planted on a corner seat, as if to reserve, unnecessarily, a place for its absent owner. And Petticate believed that he had seen the suitcase before. That was what had arrested him.

Yes, he surely couldn't be mistaken. In that horrifying instant, when Sonia, returned from the dead, had tumbled into the moving train, the case she was carrying had, by some trick of his startled nerves, photographed itself indelibly on his mind.

It wasn't at all Sonia's sort of luggage. But then the clothes she had been wearing were decidedly not her sort of clothes, either. All that was to be expected. The poor old soul had been fished out of the English Channel in a bathing suit—and naturally without twopence. She had borrowed what she could for the purpose of getting home. It was perhaps a little odd that these borrowings included a suitcase, since it was hard to see how she could have anything to convey in such a receptacle.

Still, there it was. He had no doubt whatever that the shabby-looking object on the seat was what he had glimpsed in that agonizing moment.

Suddenly he noticed that the suitcase had a pasteboard label attached to it. The thing was hanging with only a blank side exposed, but he could easily slip into the deserted compartment and see what was written on the other side. He looked up and down the corridor. There was nobody about. He pushed back the door of the compartment, walked in, and turned the label over. Printed in a straggling and uncontrolled hand he read:

Smith
116 Eastmoor Road
Oxford.

Petticate slipped back into the corridor and stood there for some moments, irresolute and scowling. What he had read was presumably the name and address of the normal owner of the suitcase. But there was the odd fact that the train was heading for Oxford now; they were just passing through Didcot, which meant that they would be in Oxford in twenty minutes. Was it possible that Sonia, in pursuance of some dreadful design against him, had actually taken on the obscure name of Smith and the resolution of going into hiding?

There was a large vague threat in this conjecture which Petticate found unnerving. It sent him, after another furtive look up and down the corridor, back into the compartment. Quickly he tried to open the case. But, although it was such a battered affair, ready indeed to give at the corners, it was nevertheless securely locked. Petticate, aware that he was now chargeable with loitering under suspicious circumstances, judged it well to waste no more time, but once more to get back into the corridor. He must simply continue his search.

And then, with an effect of great suddenness, it was over. He had entered the restaurant-car—and there she was. She was sitting facing him, and there was an empty seat in front of her. Petticate took a deep breath, walked straight forward, and sat down.

"Sonia," he said. "Sonia—dear old girl—just listen. I'll explain."

He got so far, and then stopped. He had realized that the woman wasn't Sonia. She was looking at him out of amazing dark green eyes—eyes in which he obscurely discerned that there lurked some extreme trepidation. *But she wasn't Sonia.*

Petticate was never to know how long he had sat there, speechless and staring. The woman was younger than Sonia —but not much younger. She was less good-looking—but not much less good looking. And in the coming together of these two approximations there was, he could appreciate, something that enhanced the fact of actual resemblance, both of feature and figure, to the borders of positive hallucination. But it was the eyes, the amazing likeness of those so striking eyes, that really clenched the matter. He did know, it was true, absolutely and without a flicker of doubt, that this was not Sonia. But then he was Sonia's husband.

But no! And Petticate felt the restaurant-car wheel around him, much as if it had been abruptly derailed. He wasn't Sonia's husband. Not any longer. Sonia *was* dead.

5

"I'm most terribly sorry," Petticate managed to say to the strange woman opposite whom he had sat down. "I mistook you for my wife."

"Not at all," the woman said. She spoke in a husky and gasping voice which could scarcely be habitual with her.

It seemed to Petticate that she was unnaturally alarmed. It was understandable, of course, that she should at least be disconcerted, for he had addressed her, in the first instance, face to face and having taken a full view of her. Had he said "I mistook you for an acquaintance" it might have made the incident seem a little less bizarre. Moreover, he acknowledged as his head cleared a little, he had made a tactical mistake. It wasn't, in all probability, in the least an important mistake, since he would never see this total stranger again. But it was certainly true that, in a general way, the less he said about his wife the better. There might be a danger, he could foresee, that he should come to talk obsessively about Sonia on inappropriate occasions.

"I hope I didn't startle you," he said. For some reason he had failed to stand up again and walk away after apologizing for his error.

"Not at all," the woman repeated. This time her voice was even huskier. And the teacup which she had just picked up trembled in her hand in a fashion that wasn't to be accounted for by the motion of the train. Petticate decided that she was for some reason in a bad nervous state, so that his *gaffe* had been doubly unfortunate. He was about to make his escape when the woman spoke again—setting down her cup, as she did so, with an odd air of sudden resolution.

"But you don't think I believe you, do you?" the woman asked.

Petticate could hear the breath drawn sharply in through his own teeth. They were coming too thick and fast—the jolts he was receiving on this abominable journey. He felt himself to be physically tiring. It was as if for a long time he had been plodding up some steep interminable hill.

"Believe me?" he echoed stupidly.

"You don't think I believe you, do you?" The woman repeated her identical words with a stupidity quite as striking as his own. "Or *do* you?" she added, rather as if with a desperate attempt to carry the matter farther.

"Why ever shouldn't you?" Petticate felt dimly that whimsical indignation was the right note. But he had no notion whether he had contrived anything approximating to it.

"I know all about you," the woman said. "So why pretend? Thought I was your wife, indeed!"

It was an instance of the sterling quality of Colonel Petticate's character as an Englishman that even in this most alarming turn in his affairs his powers of social appraisement did not altogether cease to operate. This woman was not, like Sonia and Mrs. Gotlop, a lady. On the other hand she was not hopelessly plebeian. She had been, perhaps, in some position which had enabled her to draw profit from the observation of her betters and could no doubt cut a genteel figure for a time if she tried—which, for the present, she was too excited to do.

Petticate felt a returning flicker of confidence. It was no doubt the result of this perception of his own superior social station. And the woman's words, he suddenly saw, were susceptible of a harmless, a merely vulgar, interpretation. She had been insinuating that his sitting down beside her on the excuse of a mistaken identification had been a subterfuge for the purpose of making some improper proposal. She thought that he had been "picking her up."

Most naturally, the delicacy of Colonel Petticate was outraged by such an imputation. But at the same time, of course, he was vastly relieved. For a moment, he had believed that he was hearing something with a decidedly sinister ring. That had been nonsense. The extraordinary circumstance of the woman's close likeness to Sonia had disturbed his judgment. All that was now needed was a display of dignity.

"Madam," he said, "I regret this incident, which is doubtless liable to misconstruction. I renew my apologies. And now you will permit me to withdraw."

The woman was not impressed.

"Your wife's dead," she said. "And well you know it."

Petticate perceived—rather as drowning men are said to perceive irrelevant things—that an attendant of whose existence he had been unaware had set before him a pot of tea, a tea-cake, a slice of buttered toast, a piece of white bread and butter, a piece of brown bread and butter, and a large cream bun. The man was now officiously pushing towards him a contraption filled with miniature pots of jam. Petticate looked at this coarse abundance rather as the condemned murderer must look at his boiled egg. Fantastic speculation flitted uselessly through his head. Perhaps Sonia had a younger sister of whom he had never heard. Perhaps that younger sister had happened to be on board that second yacht. And perhaps this was she—armed with Sonia's story, and subjecting him to this fiendish torture. Or perhaps . . .

"Your wife's dead," the woman was repeating. "And it's my belief you drowned her."

Instinct prompted Petticate to pour himself out a cup of tea. He took a scalding gulp of it.

"You had better be careful what you're saying," he managed to articulate. And he added: "Talk of that sort is best conducted in private." He had seized upon the wild thought that this woman with her fiend-like knowledge could perhaps be bought off.

"We've heard of that sort of heart attack before, haven't we? And it meant the rope for some of them that said they found the body."

Petticate took a second gulp of tea. Inevitably, it scalded worse than the first.

"I didn't drown my wife," he said, and reflected that never could a true statement have sounded so like a miserable lie. "I swear I didn't."

"Grabbed her by the ankles," the woman said. "You read about these things in the Sundays, don't you? No end of times. And tipped her up in the bath."

For a moment Petticate supposed this last astounding

word to represent a piece of slang, as when the sea is sometimes referred to as the big drink. But the invoking of the Sunday newspapers was definitive. He gave a long painful gasp.

"You think," he asked, "that I drowned my wife in her bath?"

"Oh, I know it's not what they said at the inquest— 'Enry 'Iggins." The woman looked abashed. "Henry Higgins, I mean."

Once more the train did its derailment act.

"What did you call me?" he gasped.

"Never mind what I called you. I'm not ashamed of coming from a humble home, I can tell you. There are worse things to be ashamed of than that, aren't there? You ought to know. You're Henry Higgins, and you married my aunt!"

"I did nothing of the sort." Colonel Petticate was so indignant at this imputation that for a moment he ceased being terrified. "I don't even know your aunt. We couldn't conceivably move in the same circle. And I am *not* Henry Higgins!"

"Losing your courage now, aren't you? You're a coward, Higgins, and like a coward you've acted. Giving yourself out to be a millionaire, and carrying off Auntie, and never letting her relations have a sight of either of you, and then drowning her without telling us."

"Without *telling* you!" It was dawning upon Petticate that poor Sonia's double must be a madwoman.

"Without a word of warning. So how was I to know there would be trouble over those bills? But I tell you, Higgins, if they get me, they'll get you. So you needn't come after me about that stuff. Whether you're a millionaire or not, you'd better pay up and have them ask no questions. *I'm* not frightened, I can tell you."

"There might be two opinions about that—my good woman." Petticate made these last words a sort of manifesto of recovered poise. It was clear that he and this deplorable simulacrum of Sonia had been entirely at cross-purposes, and that he had nothing whatever to fear from her. Nor, for that matter, had she anything to fear from him—although, for some reason that was still largely obscure, she seemed on the verge of panic.

He was glad to think that she was having a bad time. He very properly much resented being taken for some unrefined person called Higgins, and being by implication involved, moreover, in some web of squalid criminal suspicions and petty frauds. It sounded as if this niece of the real Higgins's late wife had found herself making criminally free with her aunt's name and credit at some awkward time after the lady's sudden decease. But Petticate wanted to make no inquiry into all that. The vagaries of low life held no charm for him. He was about to get up and walk away in silent disdain when Sonia's double forestalled him.

"Oxford," she said, as the train slowed down. "And I haven't got my bag!" She scrambled into the gangway between the tables. "But perhaps you'd like to get off here too, Higgins? What about a quiet chat with Lord Nuffield—just as between one millionaire and another?" This primitive jeer, Petticate observed, appeared to give the wretched woman as much satisfaction as if it had been a withering witticism. And she accompanied it with a defiant look from those astonishing green eyes. "Good-bye, Henry Higgins, the great industrialist. And bad luck to you!"

Petticate felt a strong impulse to lean forward and smack the woman's face. Instead, he got to his feet and bowed. This quite literal rising to the occasion probably disconcerted her a good deal more than low violence would have done. She turned and hurried away.

A few minutes later he saw her on the platform of Oxford station. Yes, she was clutching the shabby suitcase which he had endeavoured to investigate a short time ago. She was, in fact, Miss Smith. Or Mrs. Smith. And she lived at 116 Eastmoor Road—somewhere amid the dreaming spires that now began to wheel and recede as Colonel Petticate's train resumed its course westward.

It was deplorable, he reflected, that the exquisite city of Arnold and Pater should harbour so disagreeable a person.

He now found that he had an appetite. The toast was by this time cold and unpalatable, but he ate everything else. There were still a few people in the restaurant car, and he wondered a shade uneasily to what extent any of them had been aware of the contretemps in which he had been involved. But he didn't think that much could have been overheard—and, of course, it was extremely fortunate that the instinctive good breeding of which he was possessed had enabled him to terminate it on that superbly dignified note. Henry Higgins, forsooth! Colonel Petticate was now able to smile at the absurdity of the whole incident.

But he pulled himself up. It was a time, after all, for serious thoughts. He must get clear the outline of his position—of his restored position. For that was the crux of the matter: that he had got back precisely to where he was before he boarded this train and was lured into so false and dangerous a supposition by the Smith woman's preposterous resemblance to Sonia. Old Dr. Gregory had started the trouble; and to Gregory in his compartment farther down the train he must presently return.

He had allowed Gregory to see that he was upset. But Gregory had been willing to put this down to purely physiological causes, and Petticate couldn't remember that he had done or said anything to upset the idea. So far, so good. But Mrs. Gotlop was a different matter.

Yes, he had definitely put a foot wrong there. He had asked the tiresome woman, bellowing her offensive nonsense about ruddy Blimp and rural Blimp, whether she had come across Sonia on the train. Whereas he had told Ambrose Wedge that Sonia had vanished, and that he had no expectation of seeing her soon. It was an awkward discrepancy, and the more awkward because Wedge was being brought to Mrs. Gotlop's party on the following day.

Petticate finished his tea and paid his bill. It was annoying, he thought, that when he should be beginning to enjoy all the reflective quiet which the worthy and adequate finishing of *The Gates of Delight*—no, of *Man's Desire*—demanded, he should have to spend time on ironing out one difficulty after another in which his pious taking up of poor Sonia's literary burden seemed to be involving him. Still, Mrs. Gotlop could be dealt with at once. He saw precisely how to do it.

He looked out for Mrs. Gotlop as he walked back down the train—just as he had looked for Sonia, the non-existent Sonia, when he had walked up it. The eminent female biographer would almost certainly be in a compartment shared only with Johnson and Boswell. And so it proved.

Mrs. Gotlop was sitting with her back to the engine, while the two slavering brutes faced it. Johnson, who seemed more enormous than ever, was wheezing dreadfully. Boswell seemed to have rather a bad smell. Petticate, having courteously asked permission to enter the compartment, sat down between these two canine friends. Johnson eyed him with a compassionate sadness such as only bloodhounds know. Perhaps Wedge's star performer Alspach, Petticate reflected, had established his celebrated sombre tone by consorting with these creatures. Boswell, a Pekingese, looked at the newcomer in stony aristocratic contempt.

"Do you take Johnson and Boswell to the British Museum with you?" Petticate asked this question casually and cheerfully. He mustn't make too much of a business of what he was coming to.

"Certainly not. Too many *dull* dogs there. Evil communications, you know. I wouldn't have Johnson and Boswell corrupted for the world." Mrs. Gotlop made a roaring noise—rather, Petticate thought, like a pride of lions. As so often, she was amused. Anybody of nervous disposition in an adjoining compartment, Petticate added to himself, might be excused for making a grab at the communication cord.

"Then do you leave them with friends?"

Mrs. Gotlop shook her head vigorously—so that her earrings, each of which took the form of a congeries of freely moving objects, rather in the manner of what persons of artistic refinement call a mobile, clinked and clanged together to the effect of a strange music.

"Never to friends, never! They go to the Canine Clinic. Johnson has massage. But I don't know that he is benefiting. I begin to wonder whether it mayn't be a slipped disk."

Petticate contrived to look at the disgusting bloodhound with a great appearance of neighbourly affection.

"And Boswell?" he asked.

"Occupational therapy. We are a little apprehensive that there may be a latent neurosis. Boswell is encouraged to bury and unbury bones."

Mrs. Gotlop again laughed loudly, and Petticate was left in doubt whether he had been listening to a joke or to some actual, if gross, absurdity in the way of dog-mania. He wanted to say something about Boswell being encouraged not to smell, but judged that this might well give offence. So, instead, he took a plunge into the matter in hand.

"About Sonia," he said. "You remember my asking you whether you had seen her on the train? Well, I knew you hadn't. I knew you couldn't have."

Mrs. Gotlop stared. "Don't follow you, Blimp. Don't follow you at all. Why couldn't I see Sonia as well as you could? Did you take me to be blind drunk?"

"Sonia isn't on this train. She couldn't possibly be on this train. She's gone away."

"I don't blame her, if you've taken to raving. Why should you ask me if I'd seen a woman who wasn't there?"

"It was very childish, I'm afraid," Petticate said. "A sort of make believe. I was pretending that Sonia was still with me, after all."

"Do you mean that she's left you at last?"

Petticate frowned. He found Mrs. Gotlop's last two words most offensive.

"Nothing like that," he said. "Or rather, nothing *quite*

like that. But she has gone off on rather an indefinite holiday. I've no idea where to. We did have a certain mild disagreement when we were on the yacht. Close quarters like that can be a little trying, you know. So we decided on splitting up for a time. Nothing serious. But I feel a little sensitive about it, all the same. That's why I asked you that senseless question. A naive impulse to cover the matter up. Foolish of me. Of course I don't mind telling a very old friend like yourself."

Petticate's voice had rather tailed off. He was conscious that his speech had been a little too wordy. He was conscious, too, that Mrs. Gotlop had sniffed loudly. It was not, of course, a vulgar sniff of disapproval, such as might have been indulged in by a parlourmaid. It was genuinely directed to discovering whether the compartment reeked not merely of Boswell but of spirits as well. Petticate was being suspected of inebriety.

"You seem to me to be prevaricating," Mrs. Gotlop said.

"Prevaricating!" Petticate was dismayed.

"Remember my profession, Blimp. I am accustomed to discriminate between truth and falsehood as they are conveyed in the tone of a voice. Yes!"—and Mrs. Gotlop pointed a beringed finger dramatically at Petticate—"even when it comes to me muted in the pages of an old diary, a forgotten memoir. I cannot be deceived!"

"I assure you . . ." Petticate began, and then broke off helplessly. He was unnerved. Minutes had passed since Mrs. Gotlop had last roared with laughter, and this in itself was unfamiliar and alarming. But even more alarming was the absoluteness of the claim she had just enunciated. It reminded Petticate of the terrible text, bordered with forget-me-nots, which had hung above his childish cot:

[63]

I God see you. The claim was one which his conscious intellect had long ago dismissed as meaningless. Had this not been so, he might at least have been preserved from even momentarily viewing Mrs. Gotlop as one possessed of a supernatural perspicacity now.

"You cannot assure me, Blimp," Mrs. Gotlop said. "*I know.*"

Petticate took a large gulp of air—so that Johnson, who was still wheezing, turned and gave him a sympathetic glance.

"Well, yes," Petticate said desperately. "I suppose you're right in a way. I haven't been entirely candid. Sonia has been getting very restless during the last few months. Probably you've noticed it yourself. And she doubts whether Snigg's Green agrees with her health. It's quite possible that, when we do join up again, it will be elsewhere. She has heard very good reports of the Bermudas. I'm not terribly keen on a move myself. But, of course, I must stick to Sonia."

"Certainly you must. You live on her, don't you?"

The fact that Mrs. Gotlop offered this with a massive return to joviality by no means excused the woman's insolence in Petticate's eyes.

"I have my competence," he said with dignity. "I remarked as much to Ambrose Wedge earlier today, when I told him about the present situation."

"Oho!" Mrs. Gotlop gave a yell which might have been appropriate to some emergency of the hunting field. "So that's the way of it? You were going to keep quiet about this humiliating rupture at Snigg's Green—which was why you asked me that idotic question on this train. But when you heard that Wedge was coming over tomorrow, you realized the truth was bound to come out. Hence your visit to me now. My dear Blimp, what a laborious fellow you are!"

Petticate found nothing to say to this. Mrs. Gotlop had not, of course, got it quite right, since she knew nothing either of Sonia's actual death or of the false alarm of her resuscitation. But she was as securely in the target area as her limited information permitted. And Petticate certainly couldn't feel that this interview with her had been a very distinguished tactical success. It was clear that the main impression he had given was of unnecessary and unconvincing talk about his wife. And that was the very thing he knew he must avoid! He stood up.

"I must be getting back to my own carriage," he said. He spoke as easily as he could. "Gregory is there. I mustn't lose the chance of a chat with the dear old fellow."

"Tell him about your wife, Blimp, my boy."

Petticate cast about for some retort to this further impertinence, and found nothing. But his eye fell on the Pekingese.

"Do you know," he said, "I rather imagine Boswell must want to step along the corridor?"

And he gave Boswell's mistress a cold look and withdrew.

It occurred to him as he moved down the train that Dr. Gregory had probably been anxious about him. He had left the compartment in poor shape, and presumably to fulfil a need such as he had just so wittily attributed to Mrs. Gotlop's Boswell. And then he had been absent all this time. Yes, old Gregory would certainly be worried. But this proved not, in fact, to be discernibly the case.

Indeed Dr. Gregory was comfortably asleep—and he awoke only when the train slowed for the next station, the last before that at which both travellers were due to alight.

"Ah—Petticate," he said casually. "Feeling better, eh?"

"I'm entirely all right, thank you. But I thought it would be a good idea to have a cup of tea."

"Humph! And did you eat all the carbohydrate they gave you along with it?"

"Certainly not, my dear Gregory. I hold your excellent counsels too much in mind." Petticate remembered that this was true at least to the extent that he had rejected the buttered toast.

"You can pay less and eat less," Gregory said. "That's to say, if you make it clear at the start. It's an important tip."

"Decidedly it is." Petticate paused. "By the way, I saw the woman you mistook for my wife."

"Mistook for your wife? I don't know what you're talking about."

"Don't you remember telling me you'd seen Sonia at the bookstall, and that it looked as if she might miss the train?"

"Ah, yes—of course I do."

"And my telling you it couldn't be Sonia, since she'd gone off on holiday?"

"I don't remember your telling me *that*, Petticate."

Petticate looked surprised.

"Didn't I? I was almost sure I did. But perhaps I was prevented by that seedy turn."

"Perhaps you were." The quality of Dr. Gregory's interest in all this remained slight. "It was somebody like her, you say?"

"Amazingly like her. And I sat down opposite to her in the restaurant car. An odd coincidence. She even had the same eyes."

"Remarkable."

"Of course, in a sense, Sonia *might* have been on the train. That's to say, she might have changed her mind and decided to come home. But it was unlikely, if only because she's rather taken against Snigg's Green."

"I'm sorry to hear it." Dr. Gregory was too courteous an old person to say this in an absolutely perfunctory manner. But he certainly didn't go out of his way to register distress. "But I can't say I'm surprised," he went on. "A lively woman, Mrs. Petticate. And our average age is on the sombre side, round about Snigg's Green. A great deal of quiet embalming going on. I'm at it myself all day, you know—although I'd rather be bringing babies into the world than preventing a lot of prosperous semi-corpses from leaving it. Ever read Landor? Beautiful writer."

"Certainly I read Landor." Colonel Petticate, as a man of high literary cultivation, was naturally indignant at the suggestion that the *Imaginary Conversations* was not among his bedside books.

"Well, there's a bit in 'Aesop and Rhodope' that I sometimes think of having stuck up in my surgery. Something about it being better to go to bed betimes than to sit up late."

"Or to procrastinate an inevitable fall." Petticate was delighted to be able thus to cap the quotation. "But I don't know that it would persuade your patients to look round for one of the remaining killing diseases."

"Look round for another doctor, more likely." Gregory

chuckled happily. "Yes, they all keep alive—goodness knows why. Or rather, goodness knows what for? For nothing ever happens at Snigg's Green. Or does it, and am I myself too senile to be aware of it?"

"Certainly not much happens." Petticate nodded genially. "That was one of the things that Sonia said when we had our little tiff on board the yacht." He paused to be prompted. Dr. Gregory's good manners, however, were proof against such an invitation. Petticate had to plunge on, keeping it carefully light in tone. "So Sonia has gone off, you see, goodness knows where, in search of gaiety. And copy, no doubt. One must remember her work. It no doubt demands a change of residence from time to time. If I have a cable from her next week, summoning me to become an inhabitant of the Bahamas, I shall sigh. But doubtless I shall obey."

"Quite so. And I've no doubt there's excellent sailing. And golf courses like great emeralds. And air like wine."

Dr. Gregory's tone was polite and idle. But Petticate was uneasily aware of getting a searching look, all the same.

II

Sensation
in Snigg's Green

I

Colonel Petticate spent the following morning quietly at home, working on the new Sonia Wayward. He had scrapped Robert Bridges as the poet providing the book's title, and turned to Matthew Arnold:

> *'Tis all perhaps which man acquires,*
> *But 'tis not what our youth desires.*

There was about that, he considered, a sheer superbity of flatness that would afford him keen gratification when he came to see it on the title page. It would have to be explained to Wedge that Sonia had a little changed her mind. Wedge would be very unlikely to demur.

"Demur" was a delightfully literary word. Petticate doubted whether Sonia had ever used it. But it was just right for her, all the same. So he amused himself by working it into the next paragraph. "*Without demur,*" he wrote, "*the great sculptor turned on his heel.*" That was delicious. The great sculptor was, of course, Timmy Vedrenne's father. On the next page he would call him "the eminent artist." And when he made Timmy quote Byron—it would be with a quiet intensity of passion—he must remember to call Byron "the melancholy Lord of Newstead."

All this was highly entertaining, and as easy as falling off a house. The morning wore on; Petticate tapped happily away; the quarto pages of *What Youth Desires* began to litter the floor in a manner that reduced him almost to a fond nostalgia. He was saved from sentimental indulgence, however, by what was the harder part of the job: the working out of what remained obscure in the basic plot. While accepting Wedge's moral criteria, he was becoming extremely doubtful about the effectiveness of that whole business of the rowing shorts. Sonia, he felt, hadn't been quite up to her usual mark there. Perhaps he had better turn back over that first thirty thousand words and do a little revising for her. Wouldn't it be better, for instance, if the occasion of Claire's apparent discovery of Timmy in a guilty relationship was in some thematic correspondence with her first vision of him? That meant getting him stripped to the buff again. So what about a midnight bathing party—with just a little more suggestion of not wholly decorous elements than Sonia commonly ran to? One must, after all, move with the times. And it was clear enough where *they* were moving to, so far as the traditional decencies of life and art's mirror of life were concerned. . . . Petticate chuckled to himself. Yes, perhaps Wedge, in the new Sonia Wayward, should be presented with something just a titillating shade *new*.

Petticate, sitting in the pleasant bay-window of his own small study, was happily and profitably engaged in these activities and speculations when, happening to glance up and along the garden path, he observed the approach of Sergeant Bradnack.

He was being called on by the police.

The front-door bell rang. And a minute later Hennwife entered the study silently and with a long face.

"Sergeant Bradnack, sir. A summons, I'm sorry to say."

Petticate stared at his butler.

"Don't you mean a warrant?" he rather rashly asked. He regarded Hennwife as an idiot, and was always quick to correct him.

"I judge that there is no question of an arrest, sir. A motoring offence, sir. You will please excuse the sergeant for having divulged of it to me. But he hastens, he says, to cause no unnecessary apprehension."

Hennwife's employer had slumped back oddly in his chair. But now, rather unsteadily, he got to his feet.

"Well, well," he said. "No doubt Bradnack must come in and serve the thing. But it is most vexatious. I'm quite unaware of having broken any of their silly regulations. It is entirely wrong, simply to lurk and pick up one's registration. I might well have a question asked in the House. In fact, I most certainly shall."

"Yes, sir. It would be my own inclination, sir, decidedly. Shall I show the sergeant in?"

Petticate nodded gloomily.

"Yes, show him in."

Hennwife withdrew. Petticate deftly gathered up the litter of paper on the floor. If Bradnack were a detective officer of superb acumen, which he certainly was not, he might be surprised to find Colonel Petticate producing reams of dialogue. It was as well to take no risks. And he must take no risks with Hennwife and Mrs. Hennwife, either.

Bradnack came in, carrying his helmet respectfully in the crook of his arm. He was a lumbering man, and his feet were large, clumsy in movement, and heavily shod. He thus carried about with him a certain theatrical suggestion; he might have been the local grocer undertaking the part of a member of the rural constabulary in some popular diversion in the village hall.

Petticate—who had inevitably suffered, during the past few minutes, one of those exhausting alarms to which his new situation exposed him—assumed the whimsical expression and unconcerned air proper in members of the respectable classes momentarily placed in some invidious relationship with those officers of the law whom they are accustomed to regard as their hired servants.

"Good morning to you, Bradnack," he said with charitable geniality. "On the track of a crime, eh? Well, well!"

"Very sorry to disturb you, Colonel, I'm sure. And only a matter of civil misdemeanour, I need hardly say." Sergeant Bradnack, as he spoke, gazed laboriously round the study. He mightn't be looking for the traces of a crime, but he was certainly looking for something.

Petticate found himself irrationally wondering whether there was anything that he ought to have hidden away. This indiscipline of his own mind annoyed him, so that he spoke more briskly than before.

"Well, hand it over. No need to beat about the bush. And drop in on Hennwife as you go out. He'll be anxious to offer you a glass of beer."

"Much obliged, Colonel, I'm sure. But it wouldn't be regular to serve the summons on you, sir. The lady must have it herself. Apologising for troubling her, I need hardly say."

"You mean it's for my wife?"

Bradnack at this produced a blue envelope from his

pocket and studied it with care—for about the length of time, Petticate thought, in which a man might read a page of small print.

"Mrs. Ffolliot Petticate," Bradnack pronounced presently. And again he looked earnestly round the room, rather as if he supposed that Sonia might be lurking in a cupboard or behind a settee.

"My wife is not at home," Petticate said. "You had better leave the thing with me. I can give you a receipt, I suppose."

Bradnack shook his head.

"It wouldn't be regular, Colonel. We can use the registered post now, you know. But personal service can't be by deputy. I must just trouble you for Mrs. Petticate's present address."

"I've no idea of it, I'm afraid. My wife is on holiday, and moving about from one place to another. I'm quite out of contact with her."

For a moment Bradnack considered this seriously. Then an indulgent smile spread itself over his large face.

"Come, Colonel. No call to make a little game of it. The summons is nothing serious, you understand. Unnecessary obstruction. The beaks never take a severe view of that. A civil letter to their clerk, Colonel, and it won't go beyond ten bob. No call for foxing."

Petticate did not feel inclined to accept this imbecility with much tolerance.

"My good fellow, there is no question of trying to avoid the summons. I am telling you the simple truth. Mrs. Petticate is abroad, and I have no means of communicating with her. I don't know when I shall have. Her plans are quite indefinite."

"Oh, abroad!" Bradnack's face cleared. "In that case, of course, it ceases to be my responsibility, in a manner of speaking."

"I've no doubt there is a regular procedure in such cases." Petticate was again rather impatient. Bradnack had spoken with a gloomy solemnity, rather as if the tracking down of Sonia would now pass automatically to Interpol. "Your inspector will know about it."

"Yes, sir. Come to think of it, he may want a few particulars." With maddening deliberation Bradnack now produced a notebook. It was of the portentous kind that is secured by a broad black elastic band, and with this Bradnack fiddled for some seconds before bringing out a pencil. "Might I just know," he asked, "the date on which Mrs. Petticate left the country?"

Petticate was dismayed. The whole thing was, no doubt, merely tiresome and absurd. But being thus asked by the police—even in this most harmless of contexts—to account for Sonia's recent movements had its insidiously frightening side. Besides, he didn't *know* on what date Sonia had left the country. It was a detail he hadn't yet filled in. *What Youth Desires* had been too seductive. He had been inventing stuff about Claire and Timmy when he ought to have been inventing stuff about his wife.

"Only a few days ago," he said. "We had a sailing holiday together, and towards the end of it my wife decided on a trip abroad." That, he thought, was just right—neither prematurely precise nor unaccountably vague.

Sergeant Bradnack appeared much interested in this information. But his interest didn't seem to be professional in character, since he had now closed his notebook.

"That's something I've always had a fancy for," he said. "A bit of sailing. Gets you right away from it all, as a man might say. And very popular, these days, by all accounts. Dangerous, though—distinctly dangerous. Bathing, too."

"No doubt," Petticate said. The moment had come, he felt, at which it would be proper for Bradnack to withdraw.

"I've always taken an interest, now, in the bathing figures."

"Have you, indeed?" Petticate supposed, for a moment, that Bradnack was referring to those exiguously clad beauties who posture so insistently on the covers of vulgar magazines.

"Very shocking, they are. Very shocking, indeed."

"There's something to be said for your point of view, Sergeant, no doubt." Petticate was still astray.

"Take the South Coast alone, this season. Drowning fatalities. Boating fatalities. Very high, the figures are. And it's my belief that some of them are foul play."

Petticate felt a now familiar sensation of slight chill.

"It's very possible," he said.

Bradnack nodded weightily.

"That, Colonel, is just the word. It's very very possible. It's too easy. The wickedness of human nature being what it is. Mark my words, sir, there's murder in some of them boats and on some of them beaches. And sometimes there'll be no suspicion attaching. But at other times it will be otherwise. Would you happen to have seen this morning's paper, sir?"

"Not the part of it with—um—intelligence of that sort." This was true. Petticate, curiously enough, had not thought to scan those obscurer corners of his newspaper in which the discovery of drowned bodies and the like might be recorded.

"A most suspicious case, and intensive enquiries being conducted. The body washed up in nothing but bathers, Colonel, and yet the doctors are certain, it seems, that it was dead before it entered the water."

Petticate's head swam, so that Bradnack swayed before him like some vast blue weed anchored to the floor of ocean.

"Do they think," he heard himself ask hoarsely, "that the woman is identifiable?"

"Not a woman, sir." Bradnack looked momentarily puzzled. "Body of a well-nourished man in middle life. Not but what that there was a woman's body no more than ten days ago. Nibbled, it had been."

But Petticate took no interest in a ten-day-old mortality. Indeed he took no interest in anything at the moment except for his own distressing visceral sensations. He looked bemusedly round his study, until his glance fell on a side table on which stood his tantalus and glasses.

"A whisky, Sergeant, before you go?" He moved unsteadily in the direction of salvation, and a minute later was sitting in a deep armchair, gulping neat spirit. Sergeant Bradnack consumed his unexpected refreshment standing respectfully in the middle of the room. He was perhaps wondering whether the suggestion that he should consume a glass of beer with Hennwife still held good.

And at last he went away. Petticate sat for a long time, simply staring at his glass. Then he transferred his gaze to the tantalus, and stared at that. Presently he got up, walked over to the window, and raised a lower sash. He looked out. He was quite unobserved.

Petticate tipped the remaining contents of his glass into a flower bed. He brought each of the three decanters from the tantalus, and did the same with them. Hennwife might suppose that he had been going it rather heavily. But that didn't matter. What mattered was that he shouldn't have recourse to the bottle whenever an awkward moment came along. Whisky, he remembered, hadn't really helped him on board that yacht. It would help him less and less if he continued on over-familiar terms with it.

His life, he clearly saw, must now be dedicated to sober purposes. He locked up the empty decanters in their container and returned to *What Youth Desires*.

2

It was Mrs. Hennwife who brought in Petticate's chop at luncheon. She lingered after she had ceremoniously removed its little silver cover.

"Excuse me, sir—but has the mistress said what she will want to have forwarded?"

"She said that she might mention one or two things, Mrs. Hennwife, if she happened to write."

"Thank you, sir." If Mrs. Hennwife was surprised at the prospect of Mrs. Petticate's communicating with her husband being thus casually relegated to a conditional clause—and it was with the most casual ease that Petticate had expressed it that way—she didn't show it. She did, however, a little persist. "I should hardly have thought that what she took with her for a sailing holiday would be enough, sir. Not for the continent and going out."

The Hennwifes, Petticate reflected, would have to go. They hadn't been with him very long, and they were probably reasonably indifferent to his affairs. Nevertheless trouble might lurk in their continued presence in the house. Only it wouldn't do, of course, to fire them out now, or even to give them a month's notice straight away. A husband who came home without his wife and then made it his first business to pack off the servants was like one heading for a principal role in some chronicle of crime. The Hennwifes must be fitted into their due place in the phased withdrawal. The phased withdrawal was a conception in which Petticate was coming to take considerable satisfaction. It suggested so reassuringly a military commander in full control of his situation.

Or did it? Petticate bit into a morsel of his chop and frowned. There was a whole military terminology devoted to covering up disaster and dismay. And words, as Hobbes said, although wise men's counters, are the money of fools. He mustn't let a comforting phrase take the place of hard thinking.

"I quite agree with you," he said to Mrs. Hennwife good-humouredly. "Mrs. Petticate's present outfit will take her nowhere. But I suspect her of planning to make Paris an early port of call. It is where ladies have some fondness for buying clothes, I believe." He laughed carelessly. "We shall see her coming back in great style, if you ask me. An excellent chop, by the way. But this pepper mill appears to be empty."

Mrs. Hennwife, thus mildly and justly rebuked, withdrew to replenish the offending utensil with peppercorns. Petticate chuckled to himself. That had been an excellent notion about Paris. Paris, Brazil, the Bermudas, the Bahamas: he was spreading these vague and reasonable suggestions around easily and well. And the Hennwifes, although they couldn't be got rid of as quickly as he should have liked, were really no sort of menace. Hennwife himself was extremely stupid, and Mrs. Hennwife was the estimable sort of menial who appeared to have no lively interests apart from the efficient discharge of her duties.

Petticate found the pepper mill set down in front of him. But once more Mrs. Hennwife failed to withdraw.

"Excuse me, sir, but I have thought it best to tidy up a little in the mistress's room."

"Quite right, Mrs. Hennwife. I knew I had no need to suggest it." For some reason Petticate's prescient heart had sunk as he made this gracious speech. He knew instinctively that he was in trouble again. It was really astonishing how a situation like his—a situation undeniably of some little delicacy—sharpened the wits. With deliberate care, he gave a half-turn to the top of the pepper mill.

"The mistress's passport, sir. I noticed it lying on her bedroom bureau. I had wondered if it shouldn't be forwarded, sir."

"Ah, yes. Just put it on my desk, will you?" Petticate quickly took a larger chunk of chop. It would serve to occupy him until he decided what next to say—or whether to say anything.

He and Sonia had gone off without any intention of crossing the Channel or putting in at French ports. She had no doubt meant to take her passport, just in case. That, in fact, was precisely what he himself had done. But, at the last moment, she must have forgotten hers. The crucial question was simple. Did Mrs. Hennwife—or her husband, since she would presumably hand on this information to him—understand the full significance of the forgotten document? He had been representing Sonia to everybody—vaguely but at the same time definitely— as being already abroad. And she couldn't be abroad. Her passport was still here at home.

"I think, Mrs. Hennwife, that I'll have my coffee in the study, if you don't mind. And remind me at tea time

—will you?—about that passport. I might as well catch the post with it."

"Thank you, sir."

Petticate reached for the Stilton without appetite. He had strained his ears in an endeavour to determine whether Mrs. Hennwife knew or did not know that Sonia and he were supposed to be without any present means of communication. He had, after all, told Sergeant Bradnack so. And Bradnack had no doubt paid Mrs. Hennwife's husband that visit in his pantry. Petticate decided that even in Mrs. Hennwife's dim mind some disturbing thought might be at work. He had better say something more. But lightly! That, he reflected, was his cue every time.

"It's Mrs. Petticate's old passport, of course. And simply goes back to the Foreign Office."

"I see, sir."

And now Mrs. Hennwife did withdraw. Was it entirely his fancy, or had she done so with a shade of haste?

Had he said something utterly fatal?

He hadn't heard that the Hennwifes had ever been in service with persons resident abroad. Probably they knew nothing about passports. If they did, their knowledge mightn't extend to the odd fact that when one gets a new passport one keeps the old one as well, with no more than a corner mysteriously lopped from it. But, if Mrs. Hennwife was curious, there was nothing to prevent her from taking another look at the document at this moment. And even an unintelligent woman could scarcely misunderstand the plain statement that its validity extended over the next two or three years. He hadn't been too clever with that particular lie. *No* lie, it suddenly struck him, could be nearly as clever as managing to avoid having to tell one. In this particular instance, he should have been content simply to leave Mrs. Hennwife guessing— if she *was* guessing. Then, in all probability, it would pass from her mind. Whereas, if she did happen to spot the fact that he had engaged in deliberate and unaccountable prevarication, she would almost certainly pursue the matter.

After his coffee he took a turn in the garden. He was fond of it, and rather strongly felt that he had no inclination to exchange its cherished and familiar blooms for whatever outlandish stuff the Bermudas or Bahamas sprouted. Perhaps if he hung on at Snigg's Green—or quietly returned to it after, say, a year's absence—people would simply forget about Sonia: forget about her, that was to say, except as a name on an eagerly awaited title page. Perhaps he had been exaggerating the difficulties. Perhaps he should work out a bolder policy.

Puffing cigar smoke at his President Hoover roses—for he had comfortably old-fashioned ideas about dealing with pests—Petticate tried to work out this more aggressive line of action. The Hennwifes, for example. It was really intolerable that he should be rendered uneasy by them. Would it not, after all, be perfectly simple to turn them out? Would it really be at all likely, as he had rather feebly persuaded himself, to arouse suspicions of any sort? He had only to tell them firmly that he needed them no longer, assure them of excellent references, pay them a month's wages and board-wages on the spot—and that would be the end of the matter. Probably they would relish the holiday on pay before taking another situation. It was most unlikely that they would attempt to spread malicious gossip. They had always, so far as he knew, been in good service. And they understood that in superior places nobody much wants employees who have been involved in scandal.

It was after having taken a resolution to act in this sense that Petticate returned to his study to get on with *What Youth Desires*. He had locked up the typescript before going to lunch, and no doubt he had better, for the time being, continue to take that precaution. Not that the Hennwifes were at all likely to smell a rat *there*. They were accustomed to the sight of him amiably doing a bit of typing on Sonia's books, and it was inconceivable that they should penetrate to the fine distinction that he was now engaged in original composition. Of course he couldn't go on indefinitely tapping away in Sonia's absence with the Hennwifes still about the place; eventually they would come to judge his industry odd. And that was another reason for getting rid of them. He would speak to Hennwife after dinner.

Petticate entered his study and unlocked his desk. He had got out his papers before he noticed that a small slim book had been put down beside the typewriter. It had a blue cover in which there was cut an oblong window, and within the oblong window there was printed in ink his wife's name. Most of the cover was taken up with a large gilt representation of a massively uddered cow. It was the sort of book in which conservatively-minded tradesmen still render their monthly accounts. And that, in fact, was the explanation of it. It was the account-book from Sonia's diary.

But why should it have thus appeared on Petticate's desk? Petticate—oddly enough—found himself quite unable to answer this question. So he rang the bell.

It was Hennwife who appeared. The study bell was within his province.

"You rang, sir?"

"Yes, Hennwife. What in the world is the dairyman's book doing here? It's not the end of the month. And you never bring me these things, in any case."

"I beg your pardon, sir. Mrs. H. thought you would understand. I think she mentioned a matter of the mistress's passport. She said she had noticed it in the mistress's room, sir. And you asked her to put it on your desk. You offered certain observations on it, sir, if my wife was not mistaken. But of course she *was* mistaken—in another sense, that is, sir. What she remarked, as you will now see, was not the travel document she had supposed. It was *that*." And with a gesture which indubitably contained a hint of insolence, Hennwife pointed at the gilded cow.

Petticate stared at the thing. It was uncommonly like a British passport. The cow, although unnaturally square, was not, indeed, quite so square as the Lion and the Unicorn fighting for the Crown. And where a passport would have said "United Kingdom of Great Britain and Northern Ireland" this object said "Wm. Snailum, High Class Dairyman, Snigg's Green." But the resemblance was there, all the same.

It was instantly in Petticate's mind that he was confronted with alternative possibilities, each of them dire, but one decidedly direr than the other. Hennwife might be speaking the truth. Mrs. H.—as he somewhat familiarly called her—might have mistaken the dairyman's book for a passport, and discovered her error only when she went, on Petticate's instruction, to fetch it. If that were the state of the case, then he himself had offered "observations"—as Hennwife called them—that were substantially unaccountable. He had represented himself as unconcernedly aware of the fact that an absolute passport of Sonia's was indeed in her room and waiting to be returned to the Foreign Office.

But was this the likelier of the alternatives? Petticate wished he could believe so. But it entailed the supposition that Snailum's book had really been lying on the bureau in Sonia's bedroom. And this seemed scarcely plausible. Sonia took very little interest in household accounts. Nor, for that matter, did Petticate himself. It had been his habit for a long time simply to repair monthly to his butler's pantry, briefly satisfy himself that the demands made upon him were in order, and write out a number of cheques.

Petticate faced it grimly. If what Mrs. H. had seen on the bureau was *really* Sonia's passport—and that was how it looked—then either Mrs. H. herself, or her husband who was now standing here in an impassive convention of respect, was a much cleverer person than Petticate had supposed. This substitution—if it was that—of Snailum's book was a quite brilliant stroke of wickedness. It meant that the Hennwifes had Sonia's passport—her current and valid passport—in their possession. They knew that Sonia was not abroad. They knew that Sonia could not go abroad. And they were in a position to prove these facts at any time.

Petticate felt that it was time he uttered. And he re-

membered his recent judgment that even the cleverest
lies are less clever than a course involving no lies at all.

"Very well," he said. "But Snailum's book is of no interest to me. You can take it away."

"Thank you, sir." Hennwife smoothly picked up the
book. He had the superior servant's irritating trick of
offering thanks where no benefit has been conferred.
He looked at Snailum's cow, and Snailum's cow appeared
to prompt him to further speech. "Perhaps, sir, it would
be as well if Mrs. H. were to reduce the milk order by a
little?"

Petticate was irritated. He commonly was, he had been
finding, when he was frightened as well.

"Yes, yes," he said. "Let Mrs. Hennwife do as she
pleases."

"Shall you wish to continue *The Daily Telegraph* as
well as *The Times*, sir? I have noticed that you yourself seldom take up the former publication. It was the
mistress's choice. And *The Times* provides my own reading, if I may so far venture as to mention the fact, sir."

Petticate tried giving Hennwife what would be called
a stiff look. It had no distinguishable effect on the man's
bearing.

"Then you may stop *The Telegraph*," he said. "And
that weekly thing in the coloured cover."

"Very good, sir. But there is just one other matter."

"Yes?"

"The proposed oriel, sir."

"I don't know what you're talking about, Hennwife."

"It may have slipped your memory, sir. But the mistress
was talking about putting in a window of that character
in the west wall of her room. Very agreeable, it sounded

to be. And it has occurred to me that this might be the opportunity, sir—if the mistress's absence will be sufficiently prolonged for the work to be completed."

"My wife will be away a long time." Petticate snapped out this, confident at least in its truth. "But I see no occasion to begin making widows. When I want you to advise me in such matters, I'll let you know."

"Thank you very much, sir." Hennwife did his smooth bow—which Petticate imagined him to have picked up from some disgusting exemplar of his servile calling in the movies. "I note that the mistress's absence is to be prolonged."

Both the matter and manner of this irritated Petticate yet further. He sometimes imagined, too, that there were no other surviving servants in England who talked about "the mistress" in quite the Hennwifes' tiresome way. Perhaps the Hennwifes read the novels of Miss Ivy Compton-Burnett. But they were even less likely to do that than to read those of Sonia Wayward.

"Certainly a matter of months," Petticate said, with as much of crispness as he could manage. "You may tell Mrs. Hennwife as much. That's all, thank you."

"Thank *you*, sir. Mrs. H. and I must do out best to make you comfortable, sir, while the mistress is away. And I think we can undertake it, sir. Until she turns up, sir, I think we can promise to keep an eye on you. If the manner of speaking be allowed, sir."

This time, Hennwife didn't bow. He adopted the altogether unfamiliar course of giving his employer a swift glance. And then he left the room.

3

There was nothing for it, Petticate realized later that afternoon, but to go to Mrs. Gotlop's party. It was true that before tea—which had been brought to him in professionally irreproachable yet somehow sinister silence by Mrs. Hennwife—he had managed another five hundred words on Claire and Timmy. It was really *their* world, he was beginning to see, that he had a flair for. He knew that as the romance went on he would have increasingly little difficulty in shoving his—and Sonia's—characters around. His logistics would be precisely right; as the denouement approached, each of these shadowy figures, like the Corps and Divisions of some Supreme Commander's dream, would move unobtrusively and effortlessly into his or her most effective place. Whereas with Wedge and Mrs. Gotlop, with Sergeant Bradnack and the Hennwifes, things didn't appear to be working in that smooth way. Petticate was coming to realise vividly the justice of the Aristotelian distinction between the confused and refractory particulars of actual life on the one hand and the beautiful lucidity and inevitability of imaginative creation on the other.

Actual life looked—to put it frankly—like landing him

in a mess. Over his chop he had decided happily that the Hennwifes must, and could, go. Now, over his China tea and shortbread biscuits, he was confronting the gloomy possibility that it was perhaps for the Hennwifes to say whether *he* should go—and go, moreover, to some excessively disagreeable destination. Of course their present suspicions, whatever they were, could hardly be other than quite wide of the mark. They might well be imagining something entirely lurid. Like that dreadful double of Sonia's on the train, they were certainly well up in the world of Sunday-newspaper crime. Or they might be seeing the mystery—which for them consisted simply in their employer's telling unaccountable lies about his wife —merely in terms of some unedifying amatory intrigue. The only thing that was assured was their sense of having got a "handle," as they might say, upon the person whom they were doubtless accustomed to refer to as "the master" when conversing with Sonia. They had got—they not in the least fondly hoped—the master on the spot. Or at least, granted the indefiniteness of the thing, on *a* spot. And they were going to see what could be made of it.

Mrs. Gotlop's party would at least get him away from these vipers in his bosom. To one who had forsaken domestic potations, moreover—even to the rash extent of emptying his decanters—there was an undeniable attractiveness in the thought of Mrs. Gotlop's cocktails. One didn't need to yearn for what she had so coarsely called "gin galore" to acknowledge the tug, towards the end of such an appalling day, of a modest couple of dry martinis. And he couldn't go wrong on that.

He decided even to put on a dinner jacket. At Snigg's Green, as in most places nowadays, one went to cocktail parties in one's tweeds or whatever, unless it happened that one was "going on." "Going on"—the phrase palely shadowed those metropolitan grandeurs in the pursuit of which one left dinner parties upon the approach of midnight to participate in yet wilder revels—was commonly a matter of crossing the Green (for there was a real Green, and nearly everybody lived round it) to eat lamb cutlets or fricassee of chicken among faces as familiar as the fare. Petticate wasn't "going on." All too certainly, he was "going back"—to whatever the Hennwifes were, literally and metaphorically, cooking up for him. Nevertheless he would go to Mrs. Gotlop's in a stately way. It would be a sort of showing the flag.

He even put on his claret-coloured waistcoat and his claret-coloured socks. As long as his tie remained black, he told himself, he was well on the safe side of that sort of sartorial eccentricity which invites confusion with persons who play in bands. Not that Snigg's Green was very exigent in these matters. It was scarcely aware, for instance, of the solecism committed by old Sir Thomas Glyde in visiting other people's houses in a velvet smoking jacket. One bachelor might spend an evening with another, so habited. But it was surely a terrible thing, Petticate reflected, to enter a lady's drawing-room in a garment the historical associations of which were so much with clandestine tobacco in the gun-rooms of great houses in the small hours.

Petticate, as he dressed, found some satisfaction in the discovery that his mind could still pursue such familiar and significant trains of thought as these. He walked across the Green in quite a light-hearted fashion. It was seldom that he had traversed it on such occasions other than as Sonia Wayward's husband. But now he was, so to speak, Sonia

Wayward herself.

There were several cars outside Mrs. Gotlop's. That lady, despite the stigma of her literary activities, lived on the fringe of a larger society than was enjoyed by most of the Snigg's Green gentry. A scattering of people from quite far away came to her parties, and as they weren't local they could rationally be accredited as county. Petticate wasn't of course unduly impressed by this sort of thing—for Petticates, as he had often explained to his wife, were well known to have owned half Somerset, and enjoyed numerous titles of honour, until in some mysterious way they had been rather rubbed out in the course of the sixteenth century. Still, he liked the upper reaches of society. It had been one of his unspoken criticisms of Sonia that she had no talent for being in the swim.

Petticate frowned as he rang Mrs. Gotlop's bell. He kept on thinking of his wife, he noticed, in images and metaphors rather more marine than was wholly comfortable. Sonia had certainly been something of a lion-hunter—that was rather better—but the lions she hunted were literary or artistic; and they generally belonged, so to speak, to a heart of the jungle which she lacked the qualifications to penetrate. She had a vision of herself as among the eminent based on nothing more relevant than the fact that she was herself among the affluent. Could she have got hold of the austere Alspach, for instance, she would have gushed over him as a "fellow writer" at once. To Petticate, so abundantly possessed of the ordered and hierarchical view of things, this had always been embarrassing; he wouldn't himself have gushed over the President of the Royal College of Surgeons.

He could really, he reflected, go farther without Sonia

—always provided, of course, that material resources didn't fail him. So her death, although it went without saying that he judged it extremely sad, held its possibilities of what might be called social compensation.

The door was opened by Mrs. Gotlop's parlourmaid. The Petticates were the only people in Snigg's Green who maintained a married couple and thereby rejoiced in a butler; and although this wouldn't impress Mrs. Gotlop herself, it probably accounted for the respect with which Petticate was greeted by the young person in the cap.

"In the garden, sir, if you will please to walk through."

Petticate crossed Mrs. Gotlop's large low hall. Its walls were embellished in alternate sections with trophies of the chase, inherited from Mrs. Gotlop's father, and eighteenth-century engraved portraits which were understood to be associated with Mrs. Gotlop's biographical labours. There was a revolving bookcase with spare copies of Mrs. Gotlop's books, ready for autographing and presentation to particularly favoured visitors as they went away.

It was from Mrs. Gotlop that Sonia had picked up that over-expansive custom—but she had never, poor dear, carried it off with quite Mrs. Gotlop's aplomb. On top of the bookcase there was a photograph in a silver frame. Petticate had always vaguely supposed it to represent Mrs. Gotlop's deceased papa in some sort of legal wig. On this occasion, happening to look more closely, he saw that it was really Johnson, taken full muzzle and slavering. Shuddering faintly, Petticate passed out of the hall, and into the racket that was going on in the garden.

It was a racket that almost drowned Mrs. Gotlop's shouting, so that for a moment he had difficulty in locating her.

Presently, however, he did hear a mingled yapping and clinking which could have only one conjoint source, and his hostess bore down upon him, waving one bebangled arm and carrying Boswell in the other.

"Blimp!" she cried. "You poor bereft *darling!* Gin! Gin!"

Petticate, returning a somewhat coldly conventional greeting in return for this extravagance, was aware that several people—all, naturally, locals—had turned to look at him. Mrs. Gotlop could not in fairness be called a gossip. But she did carelessly fling out anything that happened to be in her head, and Petticate had no doubt that the interesting news of Sonia's indefinite holiday had travelled round the village. Quite apart from the martinis —which he blessedly saw approaching—he had been wise to come to this party. Were he to take to hiding himself away at home, much more speculation would be aroused.

"Ambrose Wedge is here," Mrs. Gotlop shouted. "There he is by the birdbath, talking to Rickie Shotover and dear old Edward Lifton. He wants Edward's memoirs, you know, only he's a little scared about the libels." Mrs. Gotlop roared with laughter, so that Boswell, to his marked displeasure, shook in her arms. "Of course you know Edward's wife? No! You absurd pet!" And Mrs. Gotlop, who had addressed this last remark to her guest and not to her dog, turned and bellowed across the hubbub of the party. "Daphne," she shouted, "come here at once! I have the loveliest man for you." She turned back to Petticate. "Be kind to the little woman," she said. "She's shy."

Petticate, much gratified that Lady Edward should thus be summoned into his presence—for the Liftons were clearly the most important guests—straightened his black tie. He was a shade disconcerted, indeed, when Lady Edward turned out to have the bulk of an armoured vehicle and very much an armoured vehicle's manner. She even scrutinized Petticate through a lorgnette, an article of polite equipment which he had supposed scarcely any longer in use except to indicate exalted rank in West End comedies. The roar of Mrs. Gotlop's laughter at her little joke reverberated in the middle distance.

"The Blues?" Lady Edward said.

The question was not phrased precisely as if it expected an affirmative answer. Petticate, however, received with complacency even an unconvincing suggestion that his background might be in the Brigade of Guards.

"My dear lady," he said whimsically, "an old army doctor—nothing more."

"Augusta Gale-Warning—who married the man Gotlop—tells me that your wife is a famous novelist. I never read novels. My husband reads them when fatigued. But he commonly choses those by the older writers. They are more reliable. Edward naturally likes to know in advance that adequate diversion is assured to him." Lady Edward put up her lorgnette again and stared through them with some fixed intent over Petticate's left shoulder. "I thought I knew them, but I don't," she said with satisfaction.

"The older writers?"

"Certainly not. Some persons who have just arrived." Lady Edward paused. "I presume, Colonel Petticate, that you and your wife move in artistic society, as poor Augusta now so often seems to do. Be so good as to give me your opinion of Mr. Gialletti."

"Gialletti?" It was with some surprise that Petticate received this apparently inconsequent inquiry. "Why, he's undoubtedly the greatest portrait sculptor alive today."

The shy little Lady Edward inclined her majestic head towards her ample bosom. "So I am given to understand. It appears that amateurs approve his work. I am unacquainted with it, naturally."

"Naturally," Petticate echoed.

"And it goes without saying that, until now, I have not met the man himself. I do happen, however, to have met his son. You know the young man?"

"I'm afraid not."

"Timothy Gialletti. Familiarly, he is known as Timmy."

"A sculptor's son? Timmy?" Petticate was vaguely troubled by the oddity of this.

"An unassuming young man with unaffected manners. I have made no objection to Claire's presenting him to me."

"Claire is your daughter?" Petticate asked, rather faintly.

Lady Edward stared at him, much as if this question had been impertinent.

"Certainly Claire is my daughter," she said. "I should have judged the fact tolerably well known."

"Ah, not in Snigg's Green." Petticate gave this disarming reply automatically. Of course he had remembered now. It was Sonia's regular habit to pick up persons and names wherever she went, and at once to tip them quite recklessly into her fiction. After each novel went in, a questionnaire regularly arrived from some lawyer apparently retained by Wedge for the purpose. And in the light of this, various precautionary changes were made in proof. It was clear that, unknown to him, Sonia had lately been in some contact with the Giallettis. But why had Lady Edward introduced the subject of the sculptor in the first place? He had better try to find out.

"Are you thinking, Lady Edward," he asked, "of commissioning Gialletti to do something? I've been told that, nowadays, he's most frightfully hard to get hold of."

"Precisely." Lady Edward Lifton now spoke with measured indignation. "Mr. Gialletti made a representation of Lifton a year ago. You may have seen it at the Royal Academy. Lifton is, of course, the head of my husband's family. But he is also tolerably well known to be the fool of it. And now Mr. Gialletti has declined to execute a similar representation of my husband, which some of my husband's colleagues in his many business enterprises are anxious to present to him. The amount of the fee, I am given to understand, is not in question. Mr. Gialletti has been pleased to say that Lord Edward has an uninteresting face. It appears that he even told his son Timothy that Lord Edward's only tolerable features are his ears. Claire, I am pained to say, judged this an acceptable pleasantry. Considering that I actually received the young man, I am bound to consider that the father's insolence in this matter falls little short of the criminal."

"I entirely agree with you." Petticate, with his proper respect for the highest ranks of society, was able to say this in all due sincerity.

Lady Edward inclined her head. Petticate supposed for a moment that she was bowing to an acquaintance straight over his—which her stature made it perfectly easy for her to do. But in fact she was acknowledging the propriety of his response to her complaint.

"And I can scarcely forgive dear Augusta," Lady Edward said, "for inviting so ineligible a person this evening. Whatever Edward may say in his easy-going fashion, a meeting with Mr. Gialletti *cannot* be agreeable."

"Gialletti—here?" Petticate stared in astonishment.

Lady Edward raised her lorgnette once more—but this time as a pointer.

"*There!*" she said.

Petticate turned. It was perfectly true. The great sculptor—the really very great sculptor—was at Mrs. Gotlop's party.

4

Lady Edward Lifton had moved majestically on. In the considerable crowd now present, there were several persons whom it would be proper for her to acknowledge. Petticate was about to seek local and less exalted society when Ambrose Wedge hove up on him.

"Well, well," Wedge said. "I didn't expect to see you again so soon." He made no attempt to render this a felicitous remark. "I heard Edward Lifton was to be here, so I allowed young Shotover to bring me over. I'm trying to persaude Lifton to do me a book."

Petticate grinned.

"Then keep away from his wife at the moment. She's not in a good humour."

"She doesn't much look as if she ever was."

"Well, she's taken particular offence at being asked to the same party as Gialletti. It seems he did Lord Lifton, and that now he won't do Lord Edward."

Wedge nodded. The mention of Gialletti seemed to excite him. "He'll do hardly anybody. The Lifton was the first Gialletti bust for years."

"Do you know, I think Sonia must have been having some contact with Gialletti and his family? But she never

[100]

told me."

"Is that so?" Wedge looked curiously at Petticate. "What a pity Sonia can't be here now."

"Yes, yes. How she would have loved a party today." Petticate found himself nervous at the mention of Sonia, although he had himself introduced her into the conversation. It pleased him, however, to manage an almost sacrilegious quotation from a lyric of Thomas Hardy's. Wedge, although professionally engaged with literature, wasn't quite the man to pick up an allusion of that sort.

Wedge looked about him. In their perfectly refined way, Mrs. Gotlop's guests were beginning to acknowledge the influence of the gin galore. Old Sir Thomas Glyde's complexion was creeping nearer and nearer to the shade of his red velvet smoking jacket.

"Yes," Petticate said, following Wedge's glance. "One day high blood-pressure will do its work, and the late Sir Thomas will be carried out amid the distressed exclamations of his *ci-devant* fellow revellers."

"Oh, I say!" Wedge looked at Petticate rather queerly. "I don't know that sudden death's all that funny. It might happen to any of us, after all. Drop down dead any minute."

Petticate amiably smiled.

"Ah, you mustn't think me callous, my dear fellow. One gets used to that sort of thing in my profession. And, if you die at a bolt from the blue, you're damned lucky, believe me. I could tell you a thing or two about the ingenuities of keeping wretches alive nowadays."

Wedge drained his rather full glass—and then appeared to wish that he had done nothing so hazardous.

"All right, all right, Petticate. But just remember your

[101]

party manners." For a moment he appeared to hesitate. "Shall I take you over and introduce you to Gialletti?"

"Please do." Petticate had drunk his two cocktails, and was resolved to drink no more. He was, he felt, at the top of his form. And there was no reason why he shouldn't try to find out just what sort of contact Sonia had been having with the sculptor. "I've a great admiration for Gialletti's work—really a very great admiration."

Wedge moved forward across the lawn.

"And does Sonia share it with you?"

Petticate, for some reason, found himself considering this question carefully.

"I'm sure I don't know. I can't remember her ever mentioning it. I should have thought Gialletti wasn't quite enough in the naturalistic manner to enchant my dear wife." For the first time that day, Petticate produced his cackle.

Wedge eyed him curiously.

"But at least she'd recognize him as no end of a swell?"

"Lord, yes. There's nobody like Sonia for knowing the exact size of lions. To have Gialletti in her menagerie would be the seventh heaven for her."

"But you say she does in fact appear to have had some contact with him?"

"Yes, indeed." Momentarily, Petticate had his now familiar uneasy feeling that he had been saying too much.

"Sonia hasn't been confiding in you, it seems."

"It seems not." Petticate tried to speak lightly. But he didn't care for Wedge's tone. It was as if the fellow were deliberately concealing something. "But perhaps we can find out."

Wedge made no reply for a moment. They were making their way through a particularly clotted group of Mrs. Gotlop's friends.

"I'm not sure," he then oddly offered, "that it would be quite playing the game, old boy."

Before Petticate could make anything of this, or decide whether it would be prudent to ask for an explanation, they were in the presence of the great man.

Gialletti was large and flabby—and he certainly wasn't of an old Huguenot family. To that extent, at least, Sonia's transforming imagination had been at work in the fabricating of Timmy Vedrenne's marble-chipping father. No doubt he did himself bang away with a hammer and chisel from time to time, but one could almost have guessed that nowadays he was happier with clay. He would have been just another elderly Italian, badly out of condition, if it hadn't been for his eyes.

These were dark under jutting brows, and they contrived to be at once brilliant and brooding. He might have been at this moment in a blaze of excitement over what was immediately before him. But as this consisted of a dozen of Mrs. Gotlop's vacantly vivacious guests, diversified only by the enormous and snuffling Johnson, it didn't seem altogether likely. The late Sir Edwin Landseer, Petticate reflected, might have found Johnson stimulating; but he didn't recall that Gialletti had ever regarded the brute creation as sculpturesque. Alternatively it might have been supposed that the eminent man was in fact immensely withdrawn upon the inexhaustible riches of his own interior vision. But, if this were so, he was at least not so lost to his surroundings as to fail to stretch out his glass whenever Mrs. Gotlop's gardener (who was disguised in a black jacket) came within collaring distance with the drinks. Petticate found this evidence of thirst infectious. He had a third cocktail, after all.

"May I introduce my friend Colonel Petticate?" Wedge asked.

"But assuredly." Gialletti managed mysteriously to add to both the brooding and the brilliance the expression of one in swift expectation of some surprising pleasure. Having risen to fame as much on the continent as in England, he had long ago acquired the expectations and accepted the responsibilities of minor royalty. He took Petticate's hand in an unexpectedly firm grip. "I am pleased to meet you, sir," he said.

Petticate was impressed. He would not, in normal circumstances, have admitted this form of words as a permissible variant upon that ejaculatory "how d'ye do" with which the well-bred Englishman instantly makes known his total lack of concern for a new acquaintance. But one had to realise that Gialletti was privileged. He was decidedly—in the amusing terminology of Petticate's favourite journal—a top person.

If Sonia had really got on speaking terms with Gialletti, it had been uncommonly deep of her not to proclaim the fact. Petticate himself, although so much more sophisticated a person than his unhappily deceased wife, would certainly have done so. If he met a Gialletti on a Monday —which he didn't often do—a good many people would be casually told of the fact throughout the remaining days of the week.

Wedge, who had also seized another drink, addressed himself to further explanations.

"Petticate, you know, is another of Mrs. Gotlop's neighbours. A hospitable old soul. She asks the whole crowd." Wedge waved his hand to indicate a number of those standing by. It didn't seem to occur to him that there was anything derogatory in this compendious description. "An interesting community, Snigg's Green."

Gialletti looked round at the company. He was habituated to a circle of people more or less staring.

"Ah, yes," he murmured. "The people are charming. The place is charming. There is a *ton*."

"They all have their points." Wedge was looking at Sir Thomas Glyde, and for a moment he hesitated, as if constrained to wonder what conceivable point such a useless and noisome old person could be credited with. "They collect pretty objects. They have knowledge of roses and of the feeding habits of tits. They visit the good poor."

Gialletti nodded indulgently. He must be very accustomed, Petticate thought, to people showing off.

"Petticate," Wedge pursued, "is an old campaigner. No man is more fascinating upon the intricate topic of tropical hygiene."

Gialletti smiled politely. At the same time he ever so slightly raised his beetling brows. It was possible to feel that a court chamberlain might advance and tactfully lead Wedge away.

Wedge patted Petticate on the shoulder—an act which the recipient of this familiarity regarded as wholly outrageous.

"But Petticate's strong suit," he continued, "is his wife. We rather think you may know her."

Gialletti bowed very slightly to Petticate.

"I am enchanted," he said, "to learn that I may have met Mrs. Petticate."

"But very probably," Wedge went on, "not as plain Mrs. Petticate."

Gialletti made a deprecatory gesture.

"Assuredly not," he said.

Wedge laughed robustly—thus making clear to everybody standing round that he had appreciated this delightful witticism.

"In fact," he said, "you have almost certainly met her as Sonia Wayward. The famous novelist, you know. One of my best authors."

"But Sonia!"

Gialletti produced this like a glad cry. A good many of Mrs. Gotlop's guests had now frankly constituted themselves an audience. And Gialletti's enthusiasm—which didn't in the least appear to be a matter of his putting on a turn—was very well received. Even those who regarded Mrs. Gotlop as the superior ornament of Snigg's Green were gratified that her principal rival was thus acclaimed by so exotic a lion as the sculptor.

Wedge, of course, was particularly delighted.

"Didn't I tell you?" he said to nobody in particular. "Dear old Sonia has been going everywhere. Quite, you know, the girl of the year."

Petticate, although displeased by this absurd description of his wife, found a certain satisfaction in thus becoming a focus of attention. Sonia, it was true, was the precipitating occasion of it. But at least Sonia couldn't butt in.

"She is here?" Gialletti—with a gesture that was at an opposite remove from Wedge's oafish back-patting—had for a moment taken both Petticate's hands impulsively in his. "She is here—your charming wife?"

"Alas, no." Petticate felt he perfectly knew how to carry off this embrace of genius. "Sonia, as Wedge knows, has gone on holiday—on rather indefinite holiday."

"I am certain she deserves it." The cordiality with which Gialletti pronounced this made it comfortably certain—despite his casting a distinguishably speculative glance on Petticate—that there was nothing double-edged in the remark. "She works so hard—no? Her books, alas, I have not read, since the reading of books eludes me. But her conversation delights me. And with her bones I am un-utterably in love."

Snigg's Green produced, at this, a perceptible gasp. It seemed, perhaps, a rather stiff dose of *la vie de bohème*. Petticate himself was startled, until his superior acumen brought him a dim sense of what Gialletti was talking about.

"My wife is professionally interesting to you?" he asked with a whimsical deference which he felt to be just right.

"The structure round the temples—it is ravishing! Ah, she is a subject, your divine Sonia."

This was so handsome that Petticate felt he must re-iterate his apologies for Sonia's not being in a position to present herself to her admirer.

"She will be terribly sorry to have missed seeing you," he said. "But she's not only taking a holiday. She's making a little mystery of it, bless her. I've no idea where she is."

Given its present context of the artistic life, this con-fession of Petticate's went down well with Snigg's Green. Sonia's supporters turned to one another with gratified smiles. Mrs. Gotlop's supporters were almost out of coun-tenance.

"But at least she will be back," Gialletti said with confidence, "by the fifteenth of October."

Petticate could make nothing of this.

"The fifteenth of October?" he echoed.

Gialletti smiled delightfully.

"But, my dear sir, you are the most modest of men! Can you have forgotten your own birthday?"

Petticate had certainly forgotten it. But he remembered, with rather a shock, that Sonia never did. The keeping of birthdays was a solemn matter with her. Gialletti's prediction had been quite reasonably grounded in her character. But how did the sculptor come to know anything about it? Despite Mrs. Gotlop's cocktails, Petticate once more experienced the now familiar sinking feeling.

"Yes," he said rather feebly, "perhaps Sonia will be back by then."

"She will be back earlier. She will be back three weeks earlier, at least." Gialletti turned roguishly to Wedge. "But our friend," he asked, "doesn't know? It is a surprise —yes?"

"I think it was meant to be." Wedge seemed slightly uneasy. "I was certainly surprised myself when you told me. And I'm not quite sure it is playing fair, you know, to let Petticate in on the secret."

This time, when Petticate spoke it was positively weakly.

"You intend," he asked, "to make a study of my wife?"

"But certainly! And perhaps it will be the last of all my portrait-busts. Sonia—your divine Sonia—I could not resist. And she has been kind enough to be enchanted. This year, she said, you should have a birthday present worthy of you."

There was a murmur of approbation and pleasure among the Waywardians. Petticate realized that his stock had never stood so high in the place before. He also realized that, if he failed to keep a tight grip on his superbly rational *Weltanschauung*, this evidence of Sonia's amiable marital disposition might become the occasion with him for some undesirably distracting uneasiness of mind. Meanwhile, he must rise to some response to Gialletti's revelation.

"I'm quite astonished," he said. "I really don't know what to say."

Here at least was the truth—and when he had added to it—not quite so sincerely—sundry cordial but not extravagant expressions of pleasure and gratitude, he could feel that, for the moment, nothing had gone disastrously wrong. Even the ill behaviour of Wedge, who seemed disposed to communicate to the world at large the amusing fact that the husband of this wifely paragon had only the day before been disposed to hint that she was quitting him for good, didn't utterly confound him.

And fortunately, just at this moment, Boswell, who had been set down by his mistress and was in consequence feeling slighted, took Lady Edward Lifton craftily in the rear and managed to bite her in the ankle. In the subsequent commotion, which included a hunt for Dr. Gregory and a telephone call to the district nurse, Mrs. Gotlop's party began to break up.

But a number of people made a point of speaking to Petticate before he went away. It was evident that any rumour of domestic disharmony that had previously got around was quite swamped and forgotten beneath the sensation caused by the news of Gialletti's undertaking. Ladies who had seen works by the master when on visits to London—or who were certain that somewhere they must have done so—assured Petticate with animation that dear Sonia was the most apt of conceivable sitters for him. If it were not that it was destined to pass into the proud ownership of Petticate himself, it would undoubtedly be purchased for the nation.

Once out on the Green, Petticate made his way somewhat reluctantly and circuitously home. Like the lowing herd, in fact, he wound slowly o'er the lea. He was very sober again, despite the cocktails. Perhaps it was because he had been given a good deal of food for thought.

5

And now Colonel Petticate began to experience more fully the mysterious ways of artistic creation.

On the morning after Mrs. Gotlop's disturbing—although in some aspects gratifying—party he found himself writing the new Sonia Wayward with the ease of one who has discovered a vein of sustained inspiration. He even evolved a technique for marvellously speeding up the work. In the morning he typed; in the afternoon he read what he had written into his tape recorder; in the evening he played this through to himself while he revised the typescript before him. This invoking of his own well-modulated voice he found extremely encouraging. It really quite brought Sonia's sort of stuff alive.

The process continued for weeks. However much he was harassed by the peculiar situation in which he had placed himself, whatever anxious consideration he had to give to every step which he must take in the actual world around him, the ideal world in which Timmy Vedrenne and his beloved trod their devious but ineluctable path towards St. Margaret's Church in Westminster remained inviolate and genially beckoning.

Moreover the new Sonia Wayward *was* just that. It

didn't, that was to say, in the least turn out to be the new, the first, Wayward-Petticate or Petticate-Wayward. His fancy for giving poor old Ambrose Wedge a jolt by gingering the stuff up, for importing into his fable some of the larger liberties recently gained for imaginative fiction, faded before the commanding fact that this was Sonia's book. It was indeed her best book. Almost from the start of his labours, Petticate had little doubt about this. It was a knowledge which afforded him much spiritual solace. He had, he realized, been a shade cavalier—not certainly towards Sonia herself, since he was far too much a gentleman for that, but to her mere mortal tenement when he had so unexpectedly found himself confronted with it on the yacht. Those fine feelings which were so nicely blended in him with a disposition inherently rational had undoubtedly given him some uncomfortable hours. But now he was making a large amends. He was putting Sonia on the map—her own mildly inimitable map—as she had never been on it before. He was so much possessed by the sense of his own piety in all this that, finding her framed photograph in a somewhat inconspicuous corner of his study, he placed it squarely on his desk beside the typewriter and regularly communed with it when some tricky moment in his narrative turned up.

Meantime he did solve, and with the utmost ease, the seemingly awkward matter of Sergeant Bradnack's mission. The summons had in due course arrived by registered post. He signed the recept for it under his own name—a proceeding to which, in a respectable household, the Post Office as represented by the Snigg's Green postman clearly had no objection at all. Then he took a little jaunt to Paris—it made a pleasant break in his devoted labours—and there ventured upon the first of what were to be his cautiously infrequent dips into actual forgery. Sonia's letter to the magistrates' clerk he considered to be a little masterpiece. It was at once dignified and respectful, and it was accompanied by a blank cheque which, upon consideration, he endorsed with the words *Under Five Pounds*. In the issue, this hint was taken in good part. The fine turned out to be thirty shillings, or no more than double what it might have been if Sonia had made her bow in court. On receiving an intimation of this, Petticate turned back a few pages of his typescript, found a convenient place, and inserted the words *Timmy sat down*. The royalties on these, he calculated, would more or less exactly cover the charge. Since the trip to Paris had been agreeable in itself, he judged it fair to pay the somewhat larger expenses of that out of his own pocket.

What Youth Desires ran so well that Petticate found, during the latter stages, that he had to give far less conscious thought to contriving his conclusion than to deciding upon just how the book was to be delivered to Wedge. The final typescript of one of Sonia's novels commonly showed a good many ink or pencil scribbles in her own hand. But to imitate this would be to go against one of the principles he had decided on: that he should cut down forgery to an absolute minimum. So, although the idea of pursuing his wife's last-moment thoughts as she read through her story strongly appealed to his artist's sense, he decided to make no manuscript alterations. It would be easy to explain to Wedge, in what need be no more than a hastily written note, that Sonia, still on her mysterious travels, had entrusted him with the whole job of preparing the final "copy" for the printer. As for proofs, she had fortunately never very much bothered her head with them. Often he had himself simply read them through for literal errors and then sent them off to press.

To Wedge, therefore, Petticate eventually wrote as follows:

Dear Wedge,

Here is our talented friend's latest. You will observe that, for her title, she has deserted Robert Bridges for Matthew Arnold. Both, I know, are favourite poets of yours. What I'm sending (as you will see, if you happen yourself to read the thing) is a very clean typescript, so the proofs should give us no trouble.

Sonia still wanders, and communication with the dear girl is intermittent. Probably I shall soon join her, shutting up shop—temporarily or permanently—here at Snigg's Green. Jamaica—or possibly Ischia—will be as good a place as another for a nice little garden from which to exclude that wolf.

Yours in haste,
Ffolliot Petticate

P.S. In the matter of royalties, please let me have a word about revising that sliding scale.

Ff. P.

Petticate read this over with considerable satisfaction before despatching it. The tone was light but the matter was businesslike. What was implied about his present relations with Sonia seemed both plausible and sufficiently dull to be unlikely to stir up in Wedge any great renewal of curiosity. The reference to the wolf, by acknowledging a slight element of cynicism in his attitude to his wife, achieved the counter-suggestion of a man with nothing very serious to hide. All in all, Petticate judged it an effective and agreeable performance.

A couple of days later he received a telegram in reply:

ms received stop willing go to twenty-five per cent at twenty thousand thirty per cent at forty thousand stop any book club etc. sales as before stop in fact would meet you any terms relying on your own business sense re scope for promotion travellers etc. stop any chance reproduction gialletti's bust ready in time for back wrapper query hope arrange dinner honour dear sonia late autumn stop alspach will preside suggest hemingway forster amis sartre proust moravia warden of all souls president of french academy delete proust apparently dead pasternak snow frost suitable guests stop wedge

Petticate read this with mingled feelings. It was rather astonishing that Wedge should put forward such excellent terms without a murmur. It was gratifying that he should have taken up the hint of a dinner in Sonia's honour, although a certain lack of sober realism pervaded the proposed list of participants. It was really too bad—Petticate thought—that the celebration could never take place. And it was equally too bad that the great Gialletti's bust would never, in fact, grace one or all of Sonia Wayward's future romances.

It was only after considerable thought that Petticate satisfied himself about a reply to Wedge's effusion. This, too, took the form of a telegram:

agree terms sonias behalf stop shall advise re bust and so delightful dinner suggestions later stop regards petticate

It was the best that could be done. But it left him with the decided sense of an awkward future. Now that *What Youth Desires* was off his hands he must get down to what was undoubtedly his next serious concern. The conception of the phased withdrawal was still far too vague in his mind. Proper definition must be given to it at once.

The first result of this resolution, unfortunately, turned out to be a grave error of judgment. It concerned the Hennwifes.

The successful termination of his first sustained effort at authorship had produced a mood of confidence in Petticate. He was a man, he had become convinced, who could bring things off. Had not Timmy and Claire—and indeed the whole thronging creation of *What Youth Desires*—done in the end precisely what he had willed them to do? It was true that he was aware of the dangerous fallacy of arguing from books to life. He had marked the contrast which unmistakably declared itself between his handling of those shadowy creatures beyond the typewriter and his handling of the Wedges and Bradnacks and Gotlops of the actual world. Still, he had proved himself a man of resource and inventiveness. He ought not to hesitate to push ahead.

The tiresomeness of the Hennwifes was something which, as he worked at the final stages of his book, he had been only intermittently aware of. But now they came much more directly into the focus of his attention. And there could be no doubt of their attitude. They believed that they knew just where their employer got off. It was true that neither of them would have used just this vulgar expression. Henn-wife himself continued to talk like a manservant in Victorian fiction. Mrs. Hennwife followed her husband more sparingly in the same idiom. But it was undeniable that they were disposed—as that same idiom might have expressed it—to the taking of liberties.

And almost more irritating than the liberties which the Hennwifes themselves took were the liberties they encouraged Ambrose to take.

Ambrose was Mrs. Hennwife's Pekingese—and a creature, to Petticate's mind, even more objectionable than Mrs. Gotlop's Boswell. For at least Boswell, however disgusting in himself, held what might be called a legitimate place in society, since his mistress belonged to a class in whom the proprietorship of small and expensive dogs is customary and allowed. How Mrs. Hennwife had come by Ambrose, Petticate didn't know; nor did he know why Sonia had admitted the animal to the house. Indoor servants may properly, perhaps, keep a cat. But a kitchen dog is an anomaly. Incidentally, it was not least where cats were concerned that Ambrose was an intolerably noisy dog. A cat in the neighbourhood aroused Ambrose to a frenzy of singularly displeasing noise. And now Ambrose was all over the place. He had established a proprietory right to the largest sofa in the drawing room. He was frequently to be observed dining in similarly unlicensed localities. He seemed particularly fond of a fresh and delicately prepared Dover sole.

In contriving such improprieties as this, perhaps, the Hennwifes were simply beginning to feel their way. If they intended blackmail, they had not yet embarked upon it. There had been no demand for money—not even veiled under an application for higher wages. On the other hand there had been a good deal of high living in what Sonia had liked to call the servants' hall. Odours of roast chicken and the like were frequently distinguishable in that quarter when Petticate himself was being sparely dieted on a slice of cold mutton. Snailum, the high class dairyman, appeared to be sending in a lot of cream. Wine was certainly disappearing from the cellar. Petticate had several times observed a nondescript woman—who proved to be a relation of Mrs. Hennwife's resident in a neighbouring village—disappearing through the back-garden gate with a loaded basket on her arm. These disorders, although they might be thought of as common form in a household without a mistress, struck Petticate as distinctly sinister. And that this was not a fanciful supposition quickly appeared. Going one day into the butler's pantry in search of an electric torch, and chancing to open a drawer that ought to contain a good deal of Georgian silver, he found that he was looking at nothing but an empty stretch of green baize.

Standing thus in what was Hennwife's stronghold, Colonel Petticate found himself trembling all over. He knew at once that this was a crisis, and one requiring both a resolute will and a clear head. He could of course take no notice. Hennwife was unaware of his visit; he could simply go away and pretend not to have made this discovery. But that would only be to defer the struggle. Soon there would be some more impudently open depredation, forcing him to fight. Better—far better—stand up to the thing now.

Petticate went to his study and rang the bell. Then he sat down at his desk, determined upon an attitude of firm composure. Hennwife entered. He had a professional way of coming into a room and, without turning round, closing the door silently behind him that Petticate had always for some reason found irritating.

"You rang, sir?"

Hennwife asked this unnecessary question in a tone no different from that which he had been employing for some time, and Petticate was now astounded that he had himself been refusing to notice its naked insolence. He found that he had to control his own voice carefully as he spoke.

"I have just come from your pantry. Can you tell me why the older silver is not in its usual drawer?"

For just a fraction of a second Hennwife hesitated. When he spoke, it was with perfect indifference.

"I have no idea, sir. No idea at all."

"You knew that it had disappeared?"

"Dear me, yes. The matter was evident, sir."

"And you said nothing?"

"I supposed, sir, that you might be entertaining your leisure by some study of it. I trust I was not mistaken."

"You supposed nothing of the sort, Hennwife." Petticate felt his face flushing. "And it is perfectly clear that the silver has been stolen."

"Very conceivably, sir. I cannot be responsible for valuable property for which provision is not made under lock and key. No well-appointed household neglects such provision. In good service, it is a thing one simply does not meet."

There was an element of truth in this which made Petticate breathe hard. He couldn't deny that he and Sonia had been careless. But this wasn't going to drive him on the defensive now.

"It is my intention," he said, "to call in the police at once." He pointed to the telephone. "Kindly get me the police station now."

[119]

At this Hennwife produced what, in his employer's experience, he had never produced before. It was a smile— and an uncommonly ugly one at that.

"I must beg to be excused, sir. It would, in my view, be highly injudicious to make any application to the police. I fear that the resulting agitation might not be good for your health. Pardon my mentioning the consideration, sir."

There was a moment's silence between the two men. Petticate realized that the battle was joined. He realized that what in fact would be injudicious would be a failure himself to pick up the telephone at once. Yet he might perhaps, without visibly weakening, defer that decisive step at least for the inside of an hour. But the thing must be done without a trace of alarm.

"Hennwife," he said gravely, "I have reason to think that you have come entirely to mistake your position in this house. I am not to be threatened. My property is not to be purloined. You may leave the room, and consult with your wife upon the very grave position in which you have placed yourself. Return in half-an-hour. If you show convincing signs of a better mind, it may be at least the means of sparing you disgrace."

The ugly smile had faded from Hennwife's face. Petticate judged that the man was shaken. He felt that he had struck just the right note with the fellow. He was pleased with himself.

And Hennwife left the room without a word. He didn't even, as was his habit, offer his employer his thanks for receiving permission to withdraw. Petticate had every hope that it was for the purpose of telling his wife that the game was up. One was always reading, after all, that blackmailers collapsed helplessly if their prospective victim stood up to them.

Petticate took a turn round his study, and then sat down and lit a cigar. He didn't precisely want a cigar; his inside wasn't quite right for it; but no doubt the action was in part a symbolical one. He was asserting to himself that he belonged to a more powerful world than that of the menial Hennwife, who had no cigars to smoke. Or at least he ought to have had none. In point of fact, Petticate's own cigars had been disappearing lately with a rather open unaccountability which went with all that high living in the Hennwife part of the house.

Petticate smoked his cigar, debating with himself the course he should next pursue. He felt he knew, as an old campaigner, that once the initiative is gained it is important to keep the enemy on the run. The Hennwifes were on the run. What power, if any, did they have of making a stand and striking back?

They had probably not, it had to be conceded, ventured as far as they had done on the strength of mere suspicion. If they believed that their employer was in the embarrassing position of endeavouring to conceal that he had been deserted by his wife, if they saw Petticate's position as merely awkward and humiliating, they might on the strength of this allow themselves a certain amount of liberty and insolence. But making off with the family silver, and then coolly advising against calling in the police, was another matter. It represented a confident wickedness for which there must be some solid ground. And Petticate couldn't have much doubt about what that solid ground was. The Hennwifes really had in their possession that current passport without which Sonia couldn't have left the British Isles.

That passport—and their story of how Petticate himself had shuffled about it—would entitle them to be heard by the law. The local police could scarcely fail to remember that Mrs. Ffolliot Petticate had written to the magistrates' clerk from Paris; and once they had put this simple two and two together they would be bound to acknowledge that there was a case for inquiry.

Petticate frowned. It was awkward, without a doubt. But at least he had got somewhere by confronting the awkwardness squarely. And now there was a tolerably simple equation to work out. Did the potential awkwardness to him, existing simply as a matter of pleasurable anticipation in the Hennwife's minds, look like outweighing the potential awkwardness to *them?*

Suppose that, as a consequence of this evil couple's going to the police, the whole truth eventually emerged. The Hennwifes might make a little money out of it. They might make, Petticate supposed, anything up to a thousand pounds by lending their names to some article in one of the vulgar newsprints. *How We Unmasked Petticate: Exclusive . . .* That sort of thing.

But the Hennwifes weren't so ignorant as to imagine that a thousand pounds is riches. And they knew the conditions of their own calling. Once they had figured as cashing in on a scandal, they were finished so far as good employment went. Nor would their position be particularly healthy even if they refrained from snatching at easy money in that way. They had delayed taking action, and in this it would be anybody's guess that their motive had been questionable. And nobody is likely to employ a married couple who have been suspected of even nursing a project of blackmail.

The conclusion of all this seemed clear to Petticate. If he stood up to the Hennwifes, if he pitched them out of the house here and now, they would probably cut their losses and vanish for good.

But suppose it didn't work out that way? Suppose that, finding themselves denied any further profit as a result of the unexpected resoluteness of their employer, they did out of sheer malignity take the risk of informing against him? In that event, just where would he stand?

It would be all up, for a start, with the new Sonia Wayward—and with all the subsequent new Sonia Waywards which he was already beginning to plan. Once active suspicion was aroused, his deception wouldn't last for a week. And that meant financial ruin, or the next thing to it. But of course his peril didn't end there. Even if he told the exact truth about Sonia's end, and even if that exact truth was believed, he had no doubt committed some crime or other in the idiotic eyes of the law. Five years for that— he seemed to hear the voice of some disgusting old judge pronouncing—and a couple of years added on for the disgraceful fraud he had proposed to perpetrate upon Wedge and the reading public of the English-speaking world. But the exact truth *mightn't* be believed. The police might persuade themselves that the course of deception upon which he had embarked had begun with murder.

Petticate had, of course, faced this possibility before in the course of his cogitations. Nevertheless it cast a fresh chill of horror over him now. Oddly enough, he felt something more than a chill. He felt a thrill as well. It was really very curious. It was almost as if, far from being a person of exceptional rationality, he was one of those abnormal beings who take satisfaction in achieving, whether in the dock at the Old Bailey or elsewhere, a notoriety quite beyond any that common mortals may hope to attain to.

Petticate put down his cigar and stared at this sudden vision of himself, fascinated. He would be in the dock—and he would be impregnable. The time had long passed when anything identifiable as Sonia's body would ever be washed up on any beach. So even if he *had* . . .

In sudden and horrible excitement, Petticate got up and paced the room. Yes, even if he had murdered Sonia, he would be absolutely safe now. Even if he told a series of lies, inventing a story of their having parted amicably, and of his having received a copy of *What Youth Desires* before Sonia's final unaccountable failure to communicate or turn up again, he would still be safe from any really dire penalty. He would insist on giving evidence—and brilliantly out-point the Crown counsel when under cross-examination. In the well of the court the Director of Public Prosecutions would be sitting glum and silent, bitterly reflecting on the folly of having tried to catch a man of Ffolliot Petticate's outstanding intellectual ability. The jury would retire for ten minutes—or would it be better fun, Petticate wondered, if they retired for ten hours?—and return a verdict of Not Guilty. There would be a murmur of applause, quickly stilled at a stern word from the judge—who would then briefly congratulate Petticate on his bearing throughout the shocking indignity to which he had been so wantonly sub-jected. Outside, reporters would be waiting. He would cer-tainly have a few words to say to the press . . .

Petticate came to himself with a jerk. He was not sure how long this strange fantasy had lasted. But he glanced at the clock and saw that the wicked and treacherous Henn-wife might return at any time. So to what, exactly, did his reflections add up?

Subservience to the Hennwifes now was surely the first step towards his own utter destruction. Once they believed that they had cowed him, they would see the green light to bleeding him white. The prospect was as black as that. Petticate paused for a moment to admire this colourful way of seeing the matter—his late literary labours had much stimulated his linguistic sense—and then went on to consider what followed from this conviction. The answer wasn't difficult. It was the old one that the Hennwifes must be defied. The Hennwifes must go.

Petticate's thought had arrived at just this point when the door opened and Hennwife entered the room once more. Mrs. Hennwife followed him. Then they both just stood, looking at Petticate silently and impassively.

It was unnerving—which was no doubt what it was meant to be. This time, Petticate stood up.

"Well," he said sternly, "have you anything to say, my man?"

Hennwife raised his eyebrows.

"Dear me, no. It was you, if I understood you rightly, sir, who wished to continue our conference."

Petticate preserved silence for a moment in face of this further impertinence. He still felt that he was in command of the situation. He turned to Mrs. Hennwife.

"And you—have you understood the need of bringing your husband to his senses?"

Mrs. Hennwife in her turn took a moment before answering. When she did so, it was with a dark obliqueness that was surprising.

"There's some," she said, "that won't come to their senses

again ever. Or that's how it looks to me."

"I suppose you imagine yourself to be talking sense, Mrs. Hennwife. But in fact you are talking nonsense—and nonsense of a kind which removes you and your husband from my employment at once. The silver which you have taken you will return forthwith. And you will then pack and go. I will make you no further payment whatever. If you feel aggrieved, I advise you to consult a lawyer. If you believe yourselves to be in possession of information which should be given to the police, you should go straight to the police station from this house. It will certainly not be to your advantage in your calling, but no doubt your duty as citizens must override that." Petticate allowed himself a tinge of irony at this point. Then he let his voice go brisk and hard again. "And now you may go."

This performance, Petticate realized, hadn't been without elements of confusion. Nevertheless he was fairly satisfied with it. He thought that it had done the trick: the simple trick, for which only a strong nerve had been required, of convincing these dastardly people that he wasn't soft. He waited for them to crawl out. He was utterly unprepared for what actually happened. Hennwife didn't retreat. Hennwife advanced. For a moment Petticate had an alarmed notion that the man actually proposed to commit a physical assault upon him. He noticed—what he had never noticed before—that this mere servile convenience (as he had always regarded him) packed a good deal of muscle beneath his dismal clothes. But Hennwife didn't in fact attack him; he merely walked past him and sat down in a large chair beside the fireplace.

Colonel Petticate was left standing in the middle of the floor, gaping at the man.

6

"I'll have a brandy, if you don't mind," the incredible Hennwife said. "Don't think I don't know where you keep it nowadays."

The astounding insolence of this, Petticate was later to reflect, might have been less devastatingly effective than it was had not the words been ingeniously humiliating as well.

During his first period of alarm before his new situation, he had, it will be recalled, passed a self-denying ordinance against solitary drinking. Later, when his resolution had first weakened and then appeared unnecessary, he had acted in what he now realised was a thoroughly bizarre fashion. Although there could be no possible objection to the Hennwifes knowing that he had reverted to his normal habits in this matter, he had in fact resumed drinking in a way that was entirely furtive and clandestine—keeping brandy and a tumbler under lock and key, and having recourse to them only when he believed himself entirely safe from observation.

This freakish conduct, he supposed, was not without a psychological foundation: every occasion upon which he took a drink was now a symbolic re-enactment of that other secret deed by which his whole present course of life had been determined. As he unlocked the cupboard where the brandy was concealed he would look round his study with the same swift apprehensive gaze as he had directed out to sea just before sending Sonia overboard.

But all this didn't make his conduct rational, and there was something peculiarly shattering in Hennwife's having detected him in so miserable an antic. So disorganized was he, indeed, that he positively felt his trembling hand going to the bunch of keys in his pocket, as if he were constrained to accept Hennwife's command like an automaton. For seconds his own will was so paralysed that he would have been forced to obey this dreadful couple even if they had ordered him to submit to some gross physical insult. But then he did hear his own voice speak—or rather he heard it desperately hiss.

"Dismissed . . . dismissed! You hear what I say? You are dismissed."

Hennwife sat back in the big chair—it came queerly into Petticate's mind that he had never seen the fellow so much as perched on a stool before—and produced a low, easy laugh.

"We weren't engaged by you, you know, and we're not going to be dismissed by you. Isn't that right, Mrs. H.?"

"Certainly it's right." Mrs. Hennwife had not moved from her position near the door, and Petticate was just collected enough to wonder whether she was inclined a little to hang back from her husband's shock tactics. "Certainly it's right," she repeated. "Everybody knows who has the say in this house—or had it until we won't be saying what. Your wife has the money, Mister Colonel Petticate; your wife engaged us; and it's your wife that will send us away again."

Hennwife produced his laugh again at considerable

length. He plainly judged this most amusing. Petticate, who found himself peculiarly outraged by a manner of address so insulting to the commission he held from the Queen, could only answer with an inarticulate gibber of rage.

"When we get a sight of her, that is," Mrs. Hennwife continued. "It's when we see Mrs. Petticate that it will be time enough to start packing our bags."

Hennwife stood up. He had apparently forgotten his demand for brandy. The ugly grin was on his face again, and he walked over to Petticate's locked bureau and tapped it.

"But just in case she's delayed," he said, "you'd better get busy on another of her rotten novels."

Petticate was never to know whether, at this, he did in fact produce a scream of fury, or whether the impulse was something strangled in his throat.

"Because, sir"—it amused Hennwife to return suddenly to his professional manner—"I fear that the calls upon your purse are likely to become heavier than of late. If you will pardon the liberty of the observation, that is to say." He moved towards the door and opened it, again in his professional, forward-facing way. He gave a nod to his wife, who went silently out. "Is there anything more, sir?"

"No!" Petticate wasn't clear what he wanted to say; he was only aware of himself as unable to produce more than this croaked-out monosyllable.

"Thank you, sir."

The door closed softly. Hennwife was gone.

Petticate's mind was numb. It was minutes before he could even begin to get into focus just what had happened, or how the situation had changed. There had been one surprise: Hennwife knew what had been going on in relation to *What Youth Desires.* Plainly he had no difficulty in dealing with a locked desk or drawer; and in this case he had shown much more ability to understand what was revealed to him than Petticate would have supposed. The man must be a professional criminal!

The implications of this were extremely alarming. It meant that Hennwife had probably not stopped short at merely examining the new Sonia Wayward while it was in progress, but had taken photographs of those pieces of the first typescript in which Petticate's manuscript corrections most clearly pointed to his being the inventor of the whole thing. This greatly strengthened Hennwife's position as a blackmailer, his ability to be really awkward if it came to the pinch.

And it did look as if it would come to that, unless Petticate gave in. If the Hennwifes were really calculating and practised crooks, they were also for some reason—Petticate could have no doubt of it—malignant enemies. If they were denied their spoils, if he didn't in fact consent to be bled white, they would find means to bring him down with no risk to themselves. And this was a fact that upset all Petticate's previous calculations. For these calculations had been based on the premise that as criminals the Hennwifes were operating on an amateur basis, and would be controlled in everything they did by the likely repercussions on their career as respectable domestic servants.

But something else—it couldn't be denied—had upset Petticate's previous calculations, too. He had sadly misfired as the man in control of the situation. He had come within an inch of accepting a ridiculous reversal of roles as between his servant and himself. He had really almost got the fellow that brandy!

Petticate shuddered at this as he positively wouldn't have shuddered in the shadow of the gallows. Indeed his mind now leant reality to this image by proposing to itself, quite firmly, that the Hennwifes must go. And not, of course, in the mere sense that he had previously intended. In *that* way, the Hennwifes had left no doubt that they had no intention of going. Well, so much the worse for them. They must *go*.

As Colonel Petticate turned this proposition over in his mind he was comforted to discover that it afforded him no qualms of conscience. His innate humanity had always revolted against the horror of long prison sentences—sentences such as convicted blackmailers always receive. And for the Hennwifes, whatever the issue of his own encounter with them, there could only be one fate waiting in the end. Sooner or later they would be caught out and locked up. Far kinder than this, surely, would be an act of more summary justice: some stroke of just retribution so swift that they would scarcely be conscious that it had overtaken them.

Having arrived at this enlightened view of the matter, Petticate went out to take a turn in his garden. The air was now autumnal and the sunshine bleak. Nevertheless there was much to gratify both the disinterested aesthetic sense and that enhanced feeling of proprietorship which he had begun to enjoy since the tragically sudden death of his wife.

The house itself was modern, but the grounds—and "grounds" was indubitably the correct word for policies so extensive in their modest fashion—had originally been those of a manor house and an adjacent manor farm. The buildings had for the most part vanished long ago. But there was still a dovecot to mark the ancient rank of the place, and a stone-roofed barn which, although much in disrepair, gave a mellow effect to the view through the small orchard.

All this made the Waywards' place enviable among the upper classes of Snigg's Green; and nothing marred Petticate's own pleasure in it except a certain injudicious fussiness of cultivation and embellishment indulged in by the former owner and not yet eradicated. Petticate was accustomed to speak disparagingly of these efforts as being suitable to what he called (in his high, old-world style) a citizen's box. There was, for instance, the fish pond. A fish pond is a delightful thing to have. But its dimensions—according to some canon which Petticate had discovered in his polite reading—ought to approximate to not less than half the area occupied by the mansion to which it belongs. His fish pond was a mere glorified affair for goldfish.

Nevertheless he walked round it with some interest now. He found himself considering it in its practical rather than its artistic or social implications. There was some two feet of water in it. And that was quite enough to drown in. The dramatist Webster—his well-stored memory informed him —presents in one of his plays the pleasing spectacle of a half-crazed cardinal who enters in the last scene muttering:

> *When I looke into the Fish ponds, in my Garden,*
> *Me thinkes I see a thing, arm'd with a Rake*
> *That seemes to strike at me . . .*

What if, here by this fish pond, he Petticate, struck at them, the Hennwifes, with a rake? And then left them face-downwards in the water?

The image thus formed before his mind brought a smile of simple pleasure to Petticate's face for a moment. But then he frowned. Of course it wouldn't do. One person may conceivably be accidentally drowned in a fish pond, even if it is only two feet deep. But not two persons. And the rake, although it would be so pleasant to use, would leave undesirable tokens of its application.

Petticate prowled on. He came to the dovecot. What if the Hennwifes, finding themselves about to be unmasked in their criminal courses, simultaneously hanged themselves here? The structure, after all, was admirably adapted to the purpose. It simply cried out—Petticate reflected as he looked up at the narrowing roof—for the spectacle of those two evil people with their toes dangling in air. And they would, of course, leave behind them some sort of confession of wrongdoing—one, naturally, that had nothing to do with Colonel and Mrs. Ffolliot Petticate.

But again, clearly, it wouldn't do. Or rather, it just couldn't be managed. Hennwife was tough. To overpower him and his foul associate severally, and then to string them up here, would be virtually impossible in itself. And moreover some act of forgery would be required which, in these circumstances, could scarcely fail to be questioned and detected.

Once more, Petticate walked on.

Dusk had fallen when he got back to the house. His limbs were aching from unaccustomed exercise, and his mouth and throat felt parched with dust. He was convinced, however, that he had found the solution of his problem.

There was still a big job ahead—particularly since he must not on any account use a saw. Of course nothing in the nature of foul play was going to be suspected. But it was not unlikely that the Hennwifes were involved in some small way with life insurance, and if an insurance company sent down some sort of investigating expert there must be absolutely nothing in the debris that might set him thinking. Parts of the massive roof of the barn had already fallen in. But most of it was intact although approaching a condition that was dangerous; and it was still entirely supported by the original structure of tie-beam, king-post and struts. He had often studied it with some care, so that he had a very good idea of the points at which he must go unobtrusively to work.

Within a week, he reckoned, and without staying in the place long enough at a time to attract suspicion, he could turn the barn into a deathtrap. As a boy he had evolved, out of cardboard boxes, sticks and a roll of string, a contraption which would come down neatly enough, at a single twitch of the hand, upon an unsuspecting blackbird or sparrow. It was something of just this sort—but this time at the pull of a stout rope—that was going to come down upon the unsuspecting Hennwifes. That he could effectively construct his trap he now had no doubt. It remained to think out some means of baiting it. Meantime he must put as much dignity and fortitude as he could into the business of sharing another and less physically threatening roof with his prospective victims.

The Hennwifes were not the less intolerable because they did, for some inscrutable reason, continue to perform their normal menial functions with a reasonable approach to efficiency. Whether this proceeded from some sense of irony entirely inappropriate to persons in their station of life, or whether it had its occasion in some motive of policy, Petticate was unable to determine. But the fact remained that his meals appeared, his rooms were dusted, and his clothes were valeted. In Mrs. Hennwife's manner there was almost nothing out of the way to be remarked. Hennwife himself, an the other hand, alternated between his normal stage-manservant's turn and savage and outrageous flights of insolence. Probably, Petticate thought, the idea was further to soften him up and utterly break him down; to keep him guessing in the sort of fashion that had proved so inimical to the nervous stability of the celebrated Professor Pavlov's dogs. There was nothing to do but resist as best he could this peculiar variety of torture until his trap was ready to spring.

And it would have been ready the sooner but for an unexpected distraction. With an altogether unexpected celerity, the proofs of *What Youth Desires* turned up from Wedge.

Petticate had much looked forward to this event. And, at a first glance, the proofs pleased him very much. There was evidence that unusual care was being given to the production and appearance of the book. And it was, after all, *his* book. Although the circumstances in which he was commencing authorship were admittedly peculiar, there seemed no reason why he should not obtain from them that sort of satisfaction which commonly proceeds from going into print in a big way. Moreover it was to be a recurrent pleasure. Definitely, although perhaps with rather less intensity, this sense of satisfaction was to renew itself year by year as the roll of Sonia Waywards increased.

It was with astonishment and dismay, therefore, that Petticate now found all these expectations betrayed. He hadn't read the first chapter of *What Youth Desires* before he was undeniably disliking the thing. Halfway through, he was loathing it.

What was the occasion of this extraordinary *volte-face?*
He asked himself the question in dismay. And the answer
seemed to lie in a consideration of his own wonderfully
complex, and therefore absorbingly interesting, personality.
Like some other outstanding men, he carried about with
him a divided mind. He had obtained great satisfaction from
writing the book, but the process had appealed entirely to
the intermittent vein of the sardonic in his composition.
Now a different impulse—which a hostile criticism might
term the purely self-regarding—was predominant in him.
He was appalled that a person of his sensibility, cultivation
and intelligence could have produced such tripe as this:
poor old Sonia's nonsense raised to a new and higher power.

He remembered indeed that poor old Sonia herself, when
she did occasionally read the proofs of one of her novels,
used to surprise him by sometimes inadvertently betraying
signs of a similar distaste. Not that she didn't predominantly
believe her stuff to be enormously good. Not that she had
the slightest settled awareness of the chasm that yawned between it and the sort of writing which has any place within
the sphere of criticism. Yet, with the print before her, she
did sometimes display tokens, poor dear, of a divine discon-
tent. It was probably something that all writers were subject to in varying degree. But its impact on Petticate himself was both unexpected and violent. And he knew, too,
that he would never now get away from it. The future was
going to be much more laborious than he had supposed.
Apart from rare moments when the original sardonic pleasure might reassert itself, he was never again going to write
a new Sonia Wayward except as a disagreeable and humiliating chore.

All this naturally didn't contribute to Petticate's nervous

ease as he continued to work discreetly on his deathtrap. But he was a resolute man, as determined that the Henn-wifes should die as that Sonia Wayward—at least in a meta-phorical sense—should live. He read the proofs with care, made a few corrections and alterations, and returned them to Wedge without any comment on Sonia's supposed present whereabouts.

And then he turned to the really tough problem of the moment.

III

The New
Sonia Wayward

I

All that was needed was a cat!

Petticate could hardly believe his good fortune when he realized that it was as simple as that. But there could be no doubt about it. Ambrose, the Hennwife's revolting Pekingese, he could make a grab at at any time—a satisfactory consequence, this, of the fact that the Hennwifes now chose to regard Ambrose and himself as having about equal rights in the house at large. If Ambrose chose to settle down for the day in the study, Petticate knew that he mustn't disturb him. Or it might be fairer to say that Petticate pretended to know this. For, of course, he was now playing his own game with the Hennwifes. Overtly he was giving every sign that he was rapidly breaking up before them. Secretly he was making his final preparations to crush them in the most literal and deeply satisfying sense.

It was cardinal to his design that, oddly enough, Hennwife himself was as attached to Ambrose as was his accursed spouse. Were the creature in distress or even mild discomfort, either of them equally would hasten to its aid. In anything suggesting crisis, they would undoubtedly hasten together.

So all that he needed was a cat. He couldn't suddenly buy

one, since he was resolved to do absolutely nothing that could attach to himself the shadow of a suspicion in the affair. And borrowing was similarly excluded. So he must simply grab a cat. Or rather—what was a little more difficult—he must put himself in the way of being able to grab a cat when the appropriate moment for the grand operation arrived.

Petticate began to study the habits of the local cats. Not many of them came near the place—presumably because of the strong dislike which Ambrose was accustomed to take to them if they did. But there was one exception to this in a large ginger or marmalade-coloured creature which did quite regularly prowl up and down an unfrequented lane immediately behind the barn. Discreet observation resulted in the discovery that it was the property of Mrs. Gotlop—from which it had to be inferred that neither Boswell nor Johnson shared Ambrose's extreme distaste of the feline species. And an equally discreet enquiry made of Mrs. Gotlop's cook, whom Petticate had fortunately been accustomed to say a few suitable words to when they met in the post office, elicited the further fact that the name of the marmalade cat was Mrs. Williams. This proved not particularly useful. When addressed as Mrs. Williams— and, even in the solitude of the lane, Petticate found some difficulty in saluting a cat in this way—Mrs. Williams paid no attention at all. When addressed less precisely under the general style of pretty pussy or the like, Mrs. Williams commonly waved her tail—which Petticate understood to be a sign of displeasure—and disdainfully moved away. He saw that the animal must be fed.

It seemed probable that Mrs. Williams shared with Ambrose a liking for good quality fish. By insincerely professing a new-born fondness for the dog, Petticate was thus able plausibly to frequent the fishmonger's and so provide himself with bait for the cat. After a number of vain attempts, in which the fish was sometimes totally scorned and sometimes eaten only after Petticate had abandoned it and left the place, he did at last begin in some measure to make Mrs. William's acquaintance. Eventually Mrs. Williams came to realize that it was worth while to keep a rendezvous with the gift-bearing Petticate every evening. After that, it looked as if it ought to be plain sailing. While feeding, the creature appeared to have no objection to being stroked. A cat that you can stroke, you can pick up and pitch into a basket. Petticate was in fact sitting on an upturned pail in the lane, stroking Mrs. Williams, and reflecting that with one full dress-rehearsal he would be ready for his bold bid for freedom, when he became aware of a phenomenon best to be described as a large warm breathing in his ear. He turned his head and found himself gazing into the eyes of Johnson: he raised his head and found himself gazing into the eyes of Johnson's—and Mrs. William's —owner. It was an awkward moment.

It appeared that Mrs. Gotlop was even more amused than usual. Her laughter had a note that was submarine and profound. When she spoke, it was to address Petticate by her customary appellation.

"Blimp!"

Petticate jumped up, so that the pail clattered under him. Disturbed by this, Mrs. Williams bounded away. Johnson put his head into the pail and made horrible snuffling noises. A scuffling in the undergrowth suggested the even more objectional vicinity of Boswell.

"Blimp the animal lover," Mrs. Gotlop expanded. "Well,

well, well!"

"Good evening," Petticate said. "It's very mild. How are your Keswick Codlins, your Ribston Pippins, your Warner's Kings?"

Mrs. Gotlop, who had no particular reputation as a keen orchardist, ignored this random attempt at rural converse. Instead, she pointed towards the ground.

"Blimp, what in the devil's name is that?"

Petticate frowned—partly because he disliked profanity or imprecation in women, partly because he resented the suggestion that the devil was at all involved in the matter, and partly because he found nothing convincing to say.

"That?" he managed. "A bit of fish, you know. Our Ambrose likes fish. And I've discovered that your Mrs. Williams likes fish, too."

"You come out and *feed* my Mrs. Williams?"

Petticate tried to manage an easy laugh.

"Yes, indeed, I hope you don't mind. Just from time to time, you know. Delightful creature, Mrs. Williams."

There was a moment's silence. Johnson, who had sat down on his massive haunches, glanced at his mistress and mournfully shook his head. Both were clearly convinced that Colonel Petticate was out of his right mind.

"And *that?*" Mrs. Gotlop asked.

Petticate saw that she was now pointing to the plate which he had taken to keeping in the barn for the purpose of serving Mrs. Williams with her fish. He now realised that it was rather an impressive plate. The Hennwifes having taken to presenting Ambrose with his meals upon the best porcelain in the house, he had been unconsciously following their example.

"Quite a pretty piece," he said feebly. "Just a single odd

plate. Found it up on a shelf."

"On the shelf yourself, aren't you, Blimp?" Mrs. Gotlop roared with laughter at her own humour. "I saw Gialletti the other day, by the way. He's looking for Sonia. He's looking for her hard. But I don't suppose he's asked *you*."

"Well, no—he hasn't." Petticate found himself continuing to cut the most wretched and unready figure before this confounded woman.

"Ah! By the way, I've heard what Ambrose Wedge has told Rickie Shotover about Sonia's new book. I'd never have believed it."

"Wouldn't you?" Petticate had the uneasy feeling of one who suspects himself to have been left in the dark about pertinent matters. "But why not?"

Mrs. Gotlop looked at him keenly. So did Johnson. So, suddenly breaking cover, did Boswell as well. It was an alarming inquisition.

"I see," she said, "you know nothing about it. More surprises, I suppose. Well, well!"

And, with a final roar of mirth, Mrs. Gotlop marched off.

Petticate found himself disproportionately unnerved by this awkward but probably insignificant encounter. He found himself contemplating an unbidden image of Mrs. Gotlop in the witness box, improbably flanked by her two canine familiars, and giving damning evidence in the sensational case of the murders in the barn. This was a senseless freak of imagination, and he saw that his nerves were getting out of control. If he wasn't going to crack up, the time had come to act.

He went back to the barn and made a final examination

of his handiwork. There was a good excuse, he reflected, for his being thoroughly nervous. The task he had achieved had been not only arduous but mountingly dangerous as well. The Hennwifes must have terrified him more than he knew in order to drive him to all this hazard. The tons of stone represented by the roof didn't yet precisely hang by a thread. But they were supported by timbers most of which had now been adequately monkeyed with in their sockets and on their corbels. He had no doubt whatever that a single heave on his rope would bring the whole impending mass thundering down.

It was now almost dark in the barn, and bats were fluttering. His nervousness increased so that, like a child, he suddenly wished the place lit up. This put him in mind of something. There was electricity laid on to one corner of the barn, and he had noticed that there was still a bulb in the socket. He mustn't grope his way to it now—that would be far too dangerous—but he must remember to take it out in the morning. It wouldn't do to have one of the Hennwifes switching it on. He didn't, somehow, fancy the prospect of even a second's naked glimpse of them as they advanced to their doom.

Petticate paused in the great wide doorway, listening. There wasn't a sound. Although he was scarcely a quarter of a mile from the centre of Snigg's Green, this part of his property was as remote as if it were buried in the country. The Hennwifes, he told himself with a satisfied chuckle, were going to most peacefully accommodated. Within twenty-four hours now they would be sleeping as soundly as any of the rude forefathers of the neighbouring hamlet.

Petticate made sure of the position of the basket into which Mrs. Williams was to be dropped. Then he returned in good heart to whatever dinner his victims had prepared for him.

Ambrose, although objectionable as a social anomaly, was an accommodating and indeed almost rational animal. On the following evening, as dusk fell, he was entirely amenable to being put on a lead by Petticate and walked through the garden and the orchard. When tethered to a post just beyond the barn, he settled down in a dignified acquiescence in whatever was going forward.

It was Mrs. Williams who gave trouble. At what was now her accustomed hour she quite failed to turn up for her refection. Petticate began to fear that Mrs. Gotlop, disapproving of the direction in which Mrs. Williams had extended the circle of her acquaintance, had confined her to the house. This would be a disaster. The whole process of cat-hunting would have to begin all over again.

At length, however, Mrs. Williams did arrive—or her eyes arrived, glinting in what was now beginning to approximate to darkness. It was some time before Petticate could make any more substantial contact. Mrs. Williams was perhaps aware of Ambrose, although he was well in the background. Or perhaps some special animal instinct warned her that matters were not as they had hitherto been. Eventually indeed she settled down to her fish. But when Petticate, with his basket ready beside him and after a cautious preliminary caress, made a firm grab at Mrs. Williams, the creature gave a quick hiss of fury, and Petticate instantly felt a sharp pain in his wrist. He had been badly scratched. He didn't however let go, and after a further second's struggle he had Mrs. Williams safely shut up. He made his way back with her to Ambrose and the barn. The

delay which had occurred was a little upsetting his calculations, and he realized that he had been foolish not to bring
a torch. He had planned his operation as an affair of the
twilight. Now it was going to take place—with an appropriateness that he didn't altogether fail to feel—in darkness.

He walked back to the barn with his burden. It proved
necessary to hurry, because Ambrose started barking before
he had covered half the ground. Mrs. Williams in her basket
was also in a state of perturbation. Petticate was sure that
he had only to set the basket down within a few feet of
Ambrose's nose for pandemonium to break loose.

The barn had a small door, commonly standing open, in
the side facing towards the house, and a larger doorway,
from which the doors themselves had vanished long ago,
directly opposite. Petticate was arranging his cat-and-dog
turn at what he judged to be a safe distance beyond this,
so that it would be natural for the Hennwifes to make
their way straight through the barn when hurrying to
rescue Ambrose. The ends of Petticate's stout rope lay
ready to his hand; it ran in a simple loop round the vital
beam he was going to bring down, and he had every confidence that he would be able to draw it clear of the
wreckage. The only real risk was that of the rope's getting
pinned under the fallen roof and so having to be abandoned
on the scene of the incident. If that happened, he would
have to get it away later, under cover of the general confusion in which rescue operations would begin.

Ambrose was now satisfactorily demented. His barking
must have carried halfway across Snigg's Green. Within
another couple of minutes Petticate, straining his ears
amid this clamour, thought that he could detect voices beyond the orchard. A moment later he was sure of it. The

Hennwifes—both of them, which was so vital a point—were behaving precisely as planned. There was no flicker of light; they must have tumbled hastily out without pausing to find a torch; and the voices indicated that, despite this, they were coming through the orchard rapidly enough. They knew the ground, after all, as well as Petticate himself.

Mrs. Williams was scratching and hissing in her basket. Ambrose went on barking. Petticate took up a light stick with which he had provided himself and gave the animal a couple of sharp cuts. Ambrose, utterly unused to this sort of discipline, at once contrived to mingle yelping with his barking as if it had been not one dog but two. Mrs. Hennwife was now anxiously calling out his name. Hennwife himself gave a couple of angry shouts, presumably with the idea of scaring off whatever enemies Ambrose was beset by.

Petticate braced himself. The supreme moment had almost come. He ought actually to be able to glimpse the Hennwifes as they passed into the barn; but if he hadn't he would at once know that they were inside from the quality of their voices. Then he must act on the instant.

But now for a moment they had fallen silent, and Petticate had an answering moment of panic in which he felt that the whole thing might go wrong. He cursed the almost entire darkness, which he hadn't in the least reckoned upon. If he mistimed that long, strong pull, and the Hennwifes were through the barn and upon him before anything happened, the resulting situation would be an extremely awkward one.

The silence—at least on the part of the human participants in the murky drama—had endured long enough to seem to Petticate wholly alarming when suddenly both the Hennwifes made themselves heard again. Hennwife was still bellowing angrily. Mrs. Hennwife was still calling out Ambrose's name. But the voices came from dead in front of Petticate, and had a resonance of which there could be only one interpretation. They were inside the barn and within seconds would be out of it again, since the direction of Ambrose's clamour must now be clear to them.

The trap had worked. Petticate felt a sudden fierce exhilaration which he knew would prove concomitant with an equally sudden access of physical strength. He dug in his heels and heaved.

2

The roof came down with so shattering a violence that Petticate for a bewildered moment supposed himself to have become coincidentally involved in an earthquake, or rather perhaps in a mingling of thunderstorm and avalanche. The ground pulsed and vibrated against the soles of his feet. The crash of falling masonry made a din suggesting the collapse not of an old stone roof but of a city. And high above this he heard, for a split and awful second, a single agonized scream.

He felt suffocated, as if the horror and terror of his deed had been too much for him. So perhaps it had. But the physical sensation, he realized confusedly, was the consequence of a dense cloud of dust that must now be hanging in the darkness around him. He experienced panic as he had never experienced it before. He felt a wild conviction that after so seismic a shock there couldn't be a window intact in Snigg's Green, so that at any moment he expected to hear a tumult of alarm from the village.

What he did hear was utter silence. Ambrose was shivering at his feet. The basket might have contained a dead cat.

He remembered that he had to remember what to do

next. There was the rope—the rope with which, so incredibly, he had brought this cataclysm about. He must grasp one end of the rope and haul it clear. He fumbled for it and pulled. At first it came away as easily as if the whole invisible length of it lay in a limp coil on the ground. And then it stuck. He heaved and heaved. The rope wouldn't budge another inch. And this somehow told him in a flash that he hadn't been quite sane about the whole thing. There had been a high probability that the rope would be pinned down like this. It could only have been a clouded mind that arrived at any other conclusion.

He dropped the rope, stooped down to the basket and opened the lid. He felt the cat—he couldn't remember its name—brush his hand as it leapt out and vanished into the darkness. He picked up the basket and threw it away. It was a battered old object, such as anybody might have abandoned in a ditch. He groped for Ambrose's lead—he did remember that the dog was Ambrose—and hitched it off its post. The job was done. He must go back to the house.

Petticate started off through the orchard, leading Ambrose behind him. Everything was still utterly and perplexingly silent. Only, in his inward ear, that single scream yet rang. Had it been a man's or a woman's voice? Had it been Hennwife or Mrs. Hennwife who had been aware for a moment of the heavens thundering down?

He let Ambrose go free as soon as they were through the orchard. He told himself that this showed that he was still capable of following out the details of his plan. It must become the theory of the thing at the inquest that the Hennwifes had gone out in search of their dog. With luck

Ambrose would now trot off to the village and be found wandering. This would be good corroborative detail.

In the house—in the empty house—a single light was shining. It came from his own study. That was where the brandy was.

They were dead. They were dead, they were dead, they were dead. He knew that this was a circumstance that conferred some enormous benefit upon him. Only he couldn't remember what it was. Did that mean that he might let it slip? He came to a halt in the darkness, knowing precisely what his situation was, and astounded that the knowledge could for a second have eluded him. It was what they called shock. Detained in hospital, suffering from shock. What if they really took him to hospital, and what if his mental state remained confused there? But that was nonsense. He only needed the brandy.

He went in through the French window. There was a fire in the study grate. Hennwife had condescended to bring in a scuttle of coal. That was over now. He must get his own coal. Until he found fresh servants. Dead, dead, dead.

He must search their things and recover Sonia's passport. He must search carefully. The Hennwifes might have had other awkward things hidden away: photographs of manuscripts, for instance. He was remembering all that clearly enough. This showed he was recovering. People might be running over from the village at any time now, he supposed. And he must have the right attitude prepared for them. But he could take the inside of five minutes for a stiff brandy.

Petticate paused in the middle of his study, suddenly uneasy. Had he heard something, seen something, *failed* to see something? What could he be failing to see? Perhaps it was only Ambrose, who of late had been so impertinently prominent in this room. He went over to the cupboard and unlocked it. He had gone on keeping the brandy locked up, even after the ludicrous exposure by Hennwife. That showed how he had been slipping into some sort of mental confusion. But he was out of it now—out of it for good. Or he would be, just as soon as he had swallowed that single big glass.

Petticate reached for the bottle. As he did so, he became instinctively aware that the study door had opened behind him. Not that he had heard it. It had been opened too silently, too professionally, for that.

"You rang, sir?"

The bottle went to the floor with a crash as Petticate swung round. Hennwife was confronting him.

Petticate had a dim feeling, as the room swayed around him, that precisely this had happened a long time before. He didn't in the least suppose himself to be confronted by a ghost. And that too was how it had been long, long ago. Not a ghost. Really . . . Sonia. For that had been it. Sonia tumbling into the corridor of a train. But of course it hadn't been Sonia. It had only been somebody very, very like her.

Perhaps this was only somebody very, very like Hennwife—Hennwife who now lay dead beside Mrs. Hennwife beneath tons and tons of stone.

Petticate pulled himself together sufficiently to look full at the thing in the doorway. But it wasn't a thing. It was really a man, and really Hennwife.

"No, I didn't ring, thank you."

[154]

The words, with an infinite strangeness, seemed to drift around the room and return to Petticate's ear. He must himself have uttered them. He remembered that, since all this began, he had several times experienced this sensation; the sensation that his own spoken words couldn't be his.

"I thought that you might have missed something, sir."

"Missed something?" This time, Petticate knew that he spoke stupidly and mechanically. His awareness was entirely taken up with the deep diabolical glee with which the monster Hennwife was indulging in his now customary torture: the torture of pretending that he was still the respectful servant.

"Your apparatus, sir." And Hennwife pointed at an empty table. "I remark that it isn't in its customary place."

Petticate stared. He did now see that something was missing. It was his tape recorder. In a flash the essence of the whole dire truth was clear to him. The Hennwifes, in their incredible malignity, had tricked him once more. They had tumbled to what he was about in the barn, and turned what ought to have been their own final tragedy into this savage piece of comedy at his, Petticate's, expense. They had recorded their own voices. They had concealed the machine, ready plugged-in, in the barn. And, at the last moment, Hennwife had slipped in, switched it on so as to begin playing back a few seconds' later, and then returned to join his wife in the orchard.

Hennwife had even thought to record that last agonized scream. . . .

Petticate was aware that he was now sitting down. He was aware that Hennwife—the other and naked Hennwife —was close to him, with a contorted face thrust into his face.

[155]

"We'll squeeze you to hell for this," Hennwife said.

Petticate made no reply. He was now listening to something else: the sound of voices hurriedly approaching the front of the house. As he had supposed would happen, Snigg's Green had taken alarm. He would have to go out with these people, whoever they were, and affect to stare in astonishment and consternation at the ruins of his barn. But more than his barn lay in ruins. His cherished plan lay in ruins as well. And here was Hennwife, still on his two feet—or were they cloven hooves?—promising to step up the torment. Mrs. Hennwife, no doubt, had gone to look for Ambrose. Petticate found himself wondering dimly whether her husband had found difficulty in persuading her to risk the creature's safety in pursuance of their fiendish counterplot. The barn, of course, might very well have come down of itself. People had sometimes had the impertinence to speak to him of its dangerous condition. But what about that fresh clean rope caught in the ruins? What about the smashed tape recorder, lying pulverized beneath the mess? With a gleam of returning reason, he realized that Hennwife would have to take care of that—and was no doubt up to doing so. Hennwife was a capable man. It seemed incredible that he, Petticate, had ever supposed him a stupid one. It certainly wasn't the Hennwifes' policy to have any immediate exposure. They believed—the vile conspirators—that they were in on far too good a thing for that.

The front-door bell rang loudly. And Petticate managed to sit up and square himself.

"Go and attend to it," he said. "Go and tell them"— and, in a manner that was afterwards to surprise him, he rose to something like a stroke of macabre humour—"go

[156]

and tell them that nothing serious has occurred."

But Hennwife, too, had his notion of fun. He was already at the study door.

"Thank you, sir," he said gravely. "Like hell," he added. And then he was gone.

Later, of course, Petticate had to join in inspecting the barn. The tiresome Sergeant Bradnack was there, in a great state of self-importance. People brought torches and lanterns, and fussed around. Most of them were yokels. But Sir Thomas Glyde—idle old idiot that he was—had turned up among them. Glyde would have to be taken in afterwards and given a drink—which meant both opening another bottle of brandy and risking Hennwife's amusing himself by some outbreak of embarrassing insolence. The business of the barn itself wasn't actually alarming. There was really nothing to be done; there was no reason to suppose that either man or beast had come to any harm in the collapse; nor could anybody express much surprise that the structure had collapsed at all. Somebody spoke knowledgeably about deathwatch beetles. Another claimant to sagacity declared that the barn, in any case, couldn't have survived the first sharp frost. Mrs. Gotlop's gardener actually stumbled over the telltale rope's end. But he was so intent upon describing to anybody who would listen the similar fate of a similar barn when he was a lad some sixty years ago, that he kicked the rope aside without pausing to look at it. So presently everybody went away; and for half an hour Petticate sat in a sort of dream in his study, watching old Glyde drinking brandy and listening to old Glyde talking nonsense. But, when the tedious old person finally went home, Petticate found that he was reluctant to let him go.

After that, he sat for a long time simply staring vacantly at the fire. He would have locked himself into his study, if the key hadn't disappeared from the damned door. He was in terror of the Hennwifes. And it was an immediate and physical terror, like that of a small boy who knows that at any moment he may be mocked or bullied or beaten at the whim of bigger boys in the next room. Strive as he would, Petticate couldn't now rid himself of this sheer morbidity.

He found himself wondering whether he could run away. Presumably the Hennwifes had to sleep. It seemed extravagant to suppose that they did so only by turns, so that there was always one keeping an eye on him. What if he were to wait till the small hours, pack a suitcase, and creep from the house? His car would start instantly; he could be beyond their reach in no time. He could be outside his London bank when it opened, draw out every penny in his current account, and then simply vanish. And of course there were two possible degrees, so to speak, of vanishing. He might vanish merely beyond any ready reach by his persecutors, or he could vanish altogether. The second was a resource that seemed utterly desperate. He would be through his ready cash very quickly—and his disappearance (apart from whatever mischief the Hennwifes might make) would engender so much suspicion that he would simply never be able to turn up again. On the other hand, merely to disappear from the view of the Hennwifes, while retaining his identity as Colonel Petticate (not to speak of his identity as Sonia Wayward) didn't look like being at all easy. In fact this whole line of thought was unprofitable. If only—if only, he told himself with sweat breaking out on his brow—he hadn't this irrational fear that his helplessness might tempt the hellhound Hennwife to sadistic outrage!

Petticate was back with this humiliating and probably irrational fear when the telephone rang on his desk.

Everything was terrifying to him now. At first he sat frozen in his chair, as if to lift the receiver would be to hear the voice of the Lord Chief Justice of England summoning him to his deserts. But the instrument went on ringing. He was even more terrified that it might bring Hennwife into the room. So he got up and made a grab at it.

"Gialletti," said a voice.

"What's that?" For a moment the name meant nothing to Petticate. He didn't even realize that it was a name. It sounded as if somebody had uttered mere gibberish.

"Gialletti. I am a sculptor."

"Yes, of course." Petticate was conscious that there had been outraged irony in the extreme courtesy with which this amplification had been offered. "What can I do for you?"

This brusque question, appropriate perhaps in the mouth of a dentist or a house agent, naturally produced a moment's pause.

"Nothing, I am constrained to fear."

"Then why the devil should you ring up?" Petticate was, of course, sadly beside himself to be speaking thus to a person of such large eminence as Gialletti. "I'd gone to bed," he added with perfectly unnecessary mendacity.

"I rang up just on the chance that you *may* know the whereabouts of your wife. She has failed to turn up for her first sitting with me. I do not understand it. It is a thing almost impossible to happen. Did I mention my name? Gialletti."

"My wife is travelling abroad. I'm afraid I can't help it if she has forgotten an appointment with you."

"But I think I can. I think that there are steps I can take. I am determined to model her. It is something I do not go back on, my dear General. Not ever."

"Well, it looks as if you'll have to go back on it this time." Not even being so casually promoted had any power to bring the desperately frayed Petticate back to civility. "May I ask if you know my wife well?"

"Not well. Hardly at all. But she delights and enchants me. Those bones, that is. I intend to find her. I intend to advertise."

"*What!*" Petticate was flabbergasted. "You mean in *The Times*—that sort of thing?"

"Of course. And in all the great journals—all the great journals of Europe and America. When it is known that your fascinating Sonia is missing from my studio—from the studio of Gialletti—all the world will go in search of her. Yes?"

"No. I mean, yes—I suppose so." Petticate again felt sweat on his brow. "But wait until—well, until a week today. I may be able to—um—to get through to her. Her last cable was from . . . from Nassau. Delightful weather, it seems. And—um—brilliant parties. A wealthy and gay society . . . How are you?"

"I am at the highest pitch of my creative inspiration. That is why I must have your incomparable wife, my dear Major. For one week, however. I will wait . . . Good-bye."

There was a sharp click, and Petticate knew that Gialletti had rung off. He put down the receiver, prepared to tumble exhausted into a chair. But he was prevented. The telephone rang again.

"I say—you must be in a deuced chatty mood, my dear chap. I've been trying to get you for ages. And by myself, too. I don't keep a secretary at home, these days. Hard times in publishing, you know. Devilish hard times."

Even without this last information, Petticate would instantly have known his interlocutor this time. It was of course Wedge. Petticate remembered inconsequently that Wedge, too, was an Ambrose. He was so exhausted that he almost asked the publisher whether he liked raw fish.

"'Hullo," he said instead. "Yes, I had somebody on the line. Fellow at the local garage. Had to go into a good deal of detail about repairing a car."

"That's funny." Wedge sounded suspicious. "The exchange seemed to get the wires crossed for a bit, and I thought I heard stuff about advertising in Europe and America."

"Quite right." Although he spoke briskly, Petticate reflected grimly on how much he had fallen from his pristine technique of never telling unnecessary lies. "Vintage car, you know. We want a set of old bronze gudgeon pins. Terribly hard to find now, it seems. We think of trying Detroit."

"I didn't think you went in for anything like that." Wedge's voice was now impatient. He evidently felt he had something important to say. "Heard from Sonia yet?"

"Well, no—not just lately."

"Then you damned well must. This can't go on, my boy. Not with what I've landed for her."

"Landed for her?" Petticate's heart sank. This could only mean trouble.

"The Golden Nightingale, my dear chap. Nothing less."

"And what the deuce is the Golden Nightingale?"

There was a strange explosion in the telephone which Petticate interpreted as a snort of contempt.

"Good God, man! You mean you've never heard of the world's biggest literary prize? I tell you I've got the Golden Nightingale for Sonia's new novel. Not, mind you, that Sonia hasn't helped. *What Youth Desires* is a remarkable book. Quite in a class by itself. My travellers were struck all of a heap by it. They see qualities in it that poor old Alspach never touched. I tell you, Petticate, it's going to be a tremendous occasion."

"A tremendous occasion?" Petticate, although naturally gratified at the effect of his Sonia Wayward on Wedge's travellers, as also upon whoever awarded the Golden Nightingale, experienced deepening alarm. "Just what, please, will be a tremendous occasion?"

"Why—the presentation of the prize, you idiot. It's going to be utterly the highlight of Sonia's life."

"I see. And just who presents it?"

"An affair called the Accademia Minerva."

"Minerva? They ought to present owls, not nightingales."

"Is that so?" Wedge appeared to be at a loss before this obscure witticism. "It's a learned society in the little state of San Giorgio, and it has enormous funds because it owns one of the casinos. Know San Giorgio? Rather the same sort of outfit as San Marino. Only it's a principality with a real live monarch. He hands over these yearly prizes himself. It's a magnificent do, I gather. Sonia will simply lap it all up. Marvellous break for the old girl."

"No doubt." Petticate, who much resented this disrespectful manner of naming his late wife, spoke without cordiality. He was, of course, inwardly appalled. Coming on top of Gialletti's demand, this further insistence that Sonia be produced—for of course it was precisely that—appeared as a last straw. But the thought of the sculptor prompted a fresh association in Petticate's mind. "San Giorgio?" he said. "Isn't that where Gialletti originally comes from?"

"Certainly it is. Glad you mentioned it. We must soft pedal on that bust for a while. Gialletti, it seems, is a fanatical republican. He hasn't been inside San Giorgio for ages, and they pretty well have a price on his head. So we can't have that bust on the platform when the Prince of San Giorgio hands over the prize on behalf of the Accademia."

"Too bad, I'm sure." Petticate, who felt strongly that about all this he couldn't care less, was by this time beyond disguising the blended rage and exhaustion that possessed him. "Forgive me if I'm not just enthusiastic about such foolery. I never much cared for comic opera myself."

"And who cares what *you* care for, Petticate? *You* didn't write *What Youth Desires*, did you?"

"Yes, I did, you damned fool."

There was a second's pause, during which Petticate felt a mingled wave of horror and relief sweep over him. It was all up now. His wonderful imposture had come to an inglorious end.

"I didn't hear what you said, Petticate. Don't get so excited. Relax. Take yourself less seriously." Wedge, who was clearly speaking the truth about not having picked

[163]

up Petticate's almost fatal outburst, was now soothing and heavily reasonable. "After all, my dear fellow, it is Sonia's show. Of course you have very superior notions about literature, and all that sort of thing. But no need to bite the hand that feeds you, eh? And the Accademia Minerva is proposing to do just that—and pretty handsomely, too. So get hold of Sonia as soon as you can, there's a good fellow. Night-night."

"Night-night." Petticate felt himself now at such an extremity of helplessness and dismay that he repeated this atrociously vulgar valediction simply without noticing it. Then he replaced the receiver and tumbled with a groan into a chair.

For a long time his mind was a blank. Nothing, that is to say, that could be called thought took place there. He was aware of nothing except a brutish and static terror. He did just obscurely know that when he *did* begin to think it could be only to review the several reasons why he was hopelessly trapped.

But presently pictures began to form themselves in his head. They were of no practical utility, since they were simply of a succession of totally improbable horrors befalling the Hennwifes. Gialletti was a threat: he had presented a sort of seven-day ultimatum. Wedge was a threat: he had presented an ultimatum only slightly more elastic. But the Hennwifes were both a threat and an object of intense hatred. Petticate didn't find himself imagining Gialletti suddenly blinded in some painful accident and incapacitated from ever handling a lump of clay again. He didn't imagine Wedge suddenly struck demented and carried screaming and for good to an asylum. He didn't even imagine the tiny state of San Giorgio and all its casinos obliterated by an earthquake or buried beneath the boiling lava of a volcanic eruption. But he did imagine what the Hennwifes would look like while succumbing to some dreadful pestilence, or brought to the gallows for some long-concealed crime, or suffering in the torture chambers of a revived Gestapo or Inquisition. And these pictures, although extravagantly improbable wish-fulfilments, did a little help him to compose his sadly jangled spirits. Slowly and as the small hours wore on—for he continued to sit before his dead fire with only the vaguest sense of time—milder imaginations took the place of these lurid ones. Eventually he found himself involved in the simplest and most pleasant—yes, most pleasant—of daydreams. Sonia had come back again.

They went to Gialletti's studio together, and afterwards dined in some long-familiar restaurant in Soho. They went across to Mrs. Gotlop's for drinks, and laughed at the absurd scandals they guessed had been put out about them. They went to San Giorgio—and after the grand prize-giving Petticate had the most amicable of chats with the Prince.

And the Hennwifes? Petticate imagined Sonia walking casually into the house and instantly dismissing them. He saw their faces, utterly confounded before the knowledge that their foul suspicions had been cobweb and their hopes of blackmail a mere fatuity. He saw them piling their shabby luggage into the Snigg's Green taxi and departing miserably to whatever low employment was open to disgraced menials without a "reference." This particular vision was so agreeable to Petticate that he presently found himself resenting intensely the one fact that made its realization impossible. Sonia *couldn't* come back. She *wouldn't* come back. It was thoroughly disobliging of her.

Only the exceptional strains to which he had been subjected in the past few hours could have reduced Petticate —normally so splendidly rational—to this pitiable travesty of thought. But, once launched upon it, he plunged further into absurdity. He didn't, after all, ask for the old girl back for keeps. That, of course, would have its advantages; she could get on with the rubbishy novel-writing against which he himself had experienced so sharp and unexpected a revulsion. But he didn't ask for that. Just a few weeks would do—and it would be only decent of her to oblige him thus far. Hadn't he always been a good husband?

Petticate stirred a little in his chair, dimly conscious that the room was becoming chilly. The inside of a month would do: to cook the goose of the Hennwifes, pick up the Golden Nightingale, satisfy the absurd Gialletti, and organize that phased withdrawal once more—this time on a more considered and less hand-to-mouth basis. Almost, it could be managed in the inside of a week.

Suddenly Petticate found himself sitting bolt upright. This was no purposeless musing. Through its apparent irrationality his reason—his powerful reason—had been secretly at work. There was a way, after all, of bringing Sonia briefly but sufficiently back from the dead. It was dangerous. It was fantastic. It was wrapped, as to its details, in formidable obscurity. But yet it was surely a way.

And he could begin to explore it by taking the first train to Oxford in the morning.

3

He got out of the house before breakfast, and without the Hennwifes appearing to be aware of him. They must be pretty confident that he wouldn't simply cut and run for good. They must be pretty confident altogether. Well, there was a shock in store for them.

But at the moment there was a shock for himself. Old Dr. Gregory was on the up platform. As Snigg's Green was no more than a halt, and the platforms exiguous affairs each provided with a wooden shelter into which one could just wheel a perambulator, conversation was unavoidable. Petticate hadn't expected any neighbours to be stirring at this hour. But medical men, he supposed, were accustomed to being early birds.

"Good morning, Petticate." Gregory seemed not much interested in the encounter, nor to have heard about the collapse of the barn. "Going to town?"

"Only to Oxford. I mean to look up one or two things in the Bodleian. My military history, you know."

"Never heard of it." Old Gregory gave Petticate his familiar keen look. "Something you've been burning the midnight oil over, eh?"

"Well, yes—to a certain extent." Petticate, who knew

that he must look decidedly seedy, seized upon this explanation. "It comes of having to lead a bachelor life. But that's nearly over, by the way. I expect Sonia back any time. Just while we clear up at Snigg's Green, that is. As I think I've told you, we propose to prepare for old age by settling down in some corner of the globe with a little more sunshine."

"No doubt I shall envy you." Gregory, although he had certainly been taking in everything that Petticate had said, gave only a casual nod as he strolled off to have a word with the Snigg's Green porter. When the train came in he would then be able, without incivility, to get into a different compartment from Petticate's. Petticate thought this highly commendable. Gregory was really a civilized old person. But why had he said all that to him? Gregory, despite his air of polite discretion, would certainly scatter about Snigg's Green the news that Sonia was returning. What Petticate had done, therefore, was boldly to burn his boats. It was something he had done before, and with far from happy results. If this Oxford gamble didn't come off, the results this time would be more unhappy still. Yet he believed that he had acted out of a wise instinct in thus committing himself by these few words to a neighbour. He couldn't go back on the enterprise now. However alarming it was, it lay straight in front of him.

The train came in, and he found an empty compartment. *Smith*, he said to himself as he settled in a corner, *116 Eastmoor Road, Oxford*. It was remarkable—it was surely almost a good augury—that he had remembered the name and address. He must now try to remember more about the woman who was virtually indistinguishable from Sonia.

The most memorable fact about her, of course, was

that she had given him a terrific shock. "Your wife's dead," she had said. "And well you know it."

And then she had addressed him as Henry Higgins. Petticate recalled vividly how extremely offensive he had found the plebeian associations of that. But more had emerged. The woman had clearly done something shady and was frightened about it: something connected with pledging the credit of an aunt who had been tricked into imagining the real Henry Higgins was a millionaire. Petticate felt no interest in the details of all this. The vital point was that a woman thus obscurely involved in some squalid manoeuvre over cheques was very likely to be in chronic trouble that way. The chance of coming into a substantial sum of money as payment for a simple act of deception would probably be attractive to her. He had only to find her—and of course it was by no means certain that he could do that—and play his cards properly. She would impersonate Sonia in that sequence of short glimpses which alone were required in order to clear up the difficulties in which he had involved himself.

There was, of course, the formidable fact that this unknown and problematical woman didn't at all belong to the sort of social world typified by Snigg's Green. Nevertheless Petticate remembered an obscure impression—not now easy to give any definition to—that there was something about the woman which might make this difficulty less absolute. Had she been at one time a sharply observing lady's maid? Or had small parts on the stage? It might be something like that. Whatever it was, it did, he felt sure, make his bizarre project sufficiently feasible to take a chance on. Of course it was going to be extremely disagreeable. Nothing was clearer to him than that he had disliked the woman. But beggars, he told himself grimly, can't be choosers. And adversity makes strange bedfellows.

Petticate frowned in distaste at the implications of this second piece of proverbial wisdom. There wouldn't, at least, be any question of *that*.

Safely arrived in Oxford, Petticate drove to Eastmoor Road in a cab. It looked promising. It was hard, that was to say, to conceive of anybody who wouldn't be glad to be out of it. Whatever the beauties of this celebrated city, they didn't extend to Eastmoor Road. The drearier parts of Reading, Petticate supposed, must wear a less discouraged air. If Mrs. Smith—or was it Miss Smith?—wasn't ready for a break, she must be so stupid that she would be of no use to him anyway. It was with reasonable confidence in the acceptability of his proposals that Petticate mounted to the dingy door of No. 116 and rang the bell.

Nothing happened. Petticate looked to his left where, only a couple of feet away, a mean bay window, partially shrouded in scruffy lace curtains, peered dejectedly over a grimy little area at the dismal road. Inside, there was a small gimcrack table, on which there perched a cheap plaster statuette of a small girl holding up her skirt in the motions of a blameless pirouette; and behind this he could just glimpse a larger table littered with papers and books. He rang again.

Again nothing happened. Out of the area, however, two grubby infants tumbled. Each held a large confection anchored to a stick with which it dabbed vaguely in the direction of its mouth. Each stared at Petticate with an open gaze of fathomless speculation. Petticate, rather unnerved by this, decided to open the door and see if it was possible to walk in.

He did so. Straight in front of him was a narrow stair-case with a few patches of tattered linoleum tacked to the treads. The way to this was barred by a couple of rusty bicycles which lay at random on the floor of the small hall. Beyond these stood a young man who had apparently emerged from the room on the left. He was strikingly good-looking in a haggard intellectual way; he had long dirty hair, and a long very dirty overcoat which he somehow contrived to suggest that he never got out of. He addressed Petticate across the bicycles.

"Are you looking for somebody? I thought I heard a bell. But of course it might be the brats."

Petticate glanced behind him. The two gutter-children were now sitting in the gutter, and by good luck had suc-ceeded in directing their confections squarely into their mouths.

"I'm looking for a Miss Smith," Petticate said. He spoke uncertainly, since it always disconcerted him to feel that he was astray in his social bearings.

Before the young man could reply, a woman's voice spoke from the room on the left.

"Right at the top of the house. You'd better go up."

The voice was followed by the appearance of its owner. She was a pale and remarkably beautiful girl with dirty hair—and dressed in what appeared to be black skin-tights topped by a very bulky jacket reaching precisely to the top of her thighs. Now she was looking past Petticate to the urchins in the road.

"Marcus," she called out, "Marcus and Dominic—come inside, please."

The urchins, thus summoned with a mingled politeness

[171]

and unquestioning expectation of obedience which held social implications more bewildering still to Petticate, tottered up the steps and began crawling over the bicycles. The young man stooped and had the appearance of picking them up like puppies, each by the scruff of its neck.

"I think you'll find Susie in," he said. "There isn't much doing with her nowadays, it seems to me. What would you say, Persephone?"

"Poor old dear," the girl said. "She's not a bad sort."

"Do I understand," Petticate asked, "that you are not related to—um—Miss Smith?"

It was clear that Persephone, had she been the sort that stares, would have stared.

"Oh, no. We simply have digs here."

"Susie is very decent about the brats," the young man said. "Looks after them sometimes, if we both happen to have tutorials or lectures."

"I see." What Petticate saw was that these unkempt young people, although they had produced Marcus and Dominic and were presumably married, were in fact undergraduate members of the university. As his own notions of this institution were entirely conventional and second-hand, the realization was rather a shock. The young man might have been a *poet maudit* strayed out of nineteenth-century Paris. The young woman he simply couldn't place or type at all. "I think I'll take your advice and go up," he said. "If you will be so very kind as to move one of the bicycles."

At this the young man, who was shod in tattered gym-shoes, deftly inserted a toe in the spokes of the nearest machine and flicked it against the wall. Petticate, although he felt that this manner of complying with his

[172]

request was lacking in proper acknowledgement of his importance, spoke a stiff word of thanks and mounted the staircase.

"Susie mayn't be up yet," Persephone called after him. "But I don't suppose it will matter."

Petticate climbed the steep and treacherously clothed treads with misgiving. Just what had the girl meant by that last remark? What did the young man mean by saying that there didn't seem to be much doing with Susie nowadays? Surely . . . surely Susie Smith couldn't be an elderly harlot? Surely he, Petticate, so securely a man of the world, couldn't have missed *that* about the woman he had encountered in the train?

But again, he realized, his ideas were no doubt conventional and out of date. Nowadays, however deplorable the fact, one had to admit that there were all sorts and degrees of sexually irregular courses. And in any case it was too late to go back now. Petticate went resolutely up the final flight of stairs. There was only one door at the top, and —without pausing to consider whether his heart was sinking—he knocked at it.

"Come in!"

Now, just for a second, he did pause. He had, for some reason, expected any summons to enter that did come from beyond the door to be tinged with apprehension or alarm. Miss Smith, after all, had been full of such feelings when he had last parted from her. But this accent wasn't alarmed. It was rather cheerful.

Petticate opened the door and walked in, only to pause in dismay when he was securely across the threshold. For Sonia—the woman, that was to say, who so shatteringly

[173]

resembled Sonia—had certainly not yet arisen. She was sitting up in bed, with a small tray before her. For a moment he thought with horror that, like our barbarous Elizabethan ancestors, it was her habit to sleep with nothing on at all. Then he saw that she was in fact wearing some sort of night attire, although its transparency seemed to him indecent in the extreme. He saw too that, in this aspect now revealed to him, Susie Smith was what must be called a remarkably fine woman. Rubens or Renoir would have been delighted with her. Although she wasn't perhaps much younger than poor Sonia, she was definitely in what would best be described as an earlier and more compelling phase of maturation.

Petticate almost turned and ran. He had known that he disliked the woman—but something very deep in him made him dislike her much more when he felt the strong and gross sexual attractiveness she possessed. This was extremely odd, since he was a man not without intermittent inclinations to venery. But if odd it was absolute. He knew—after this vision amid the bedclothes—that the physical presence of Miss Smith would never be other than alarming to him.

Miss Smith, once more, was not herself alarmed. She put down her cup and stared at Petticate in amused astonishment.

"Well," she said, "if it isn't *you!*"

4

"And if it isn't nice to see you again!" Susie Smith went on easily. "I was a bit under the weather, wasn't I, that last time? All that about Auntie and Higgins. And it looking as if the police might get interested in those cheques. But all's well that ends well."

Petticate didn't manage to speak. Susie looked at him sharply. Then she leaned far out of her bed, so that his scandalised gaze was treated to further expanses of near-nudity. What she was doing, however, was to reach for a dressing gown in which she now modestly encased herself. She was in her vulgar fashion, he could see, a woman of rapid discernment, who had tumbled to the fact of his being shocked.

"Yes," she went on comfortably, "I was in a bad way on that train. Taking you for somebody called Henry Higgins! Where was my social sense? And you seemed offended, all right. So fancy your turning up again. It's a small world."

Petticate was staring at her, fascinated. Was the thing conceivably possible? Susie Smith was *much* more vulgar than he had supposed. On the other hand, he now had an impression that she was also much more clever.

"Is it just a call?" Susie asked. "The time of day, in a manner of speaking? Give me a cigarette, dearie."

Petticate brought out his cigarette case and stepped forward. "No, not just a call," he said. He tried to reach back into his memory for the right tone to strike with a Susie Smith. "A little matter of business as well."

Susie drew herself back on her pillow and looked at him severely.

"No coarse talk, if you please. Still—you can give me a light."

Petticate struck a match, and decided to plunge.

"Listen," he said. "It's like this. I want you to be my wife. I mean, I want you to take my wife's place, just for a week or two. You're the split image of her."

"So everybody tells me."

"What's that?" Petticate was startled. "What do you know about it?"

Once more Susie reached out of bed, this time to a small bookcase. "Sonia Wayward," she said. "Her picture's on the back of her books, isn't it? Half-a-crown, I paid for this one. Poor reading, if you ask me. But it makes money, I'll answer for it." She had produced a paper-backed novel. "It's a likeness, all right. Particularly above the neck. Which is what most people notice, I don't doubt. It must have been what you were noticing when you behaved funny on that train . . . Colonel Petticate." Susie had plainly picked up this name from the little biographical blurb under Sonia's photograph. "But why do you want me to take your wife's place? It sounds a bit crazy to me."

"I don't know that I need explain in great detail." It seemed to Petticate that he must make it quite clear from the start that Susie was simply to play a hireling's role.

"What worries me is whether you can do it. Do you know much about ladies?"

As far as he could see, Susie Smith accepted this question without offence.

"Well," she said, "I know quite a lot about gentlemen." She paused. "I had to," she added a shade grimly.

Petticate was embarrassed. It could scarcely be doubted now that Susie's past was not one of unimpaired moral integrity.

"I'm afraid," he said, "that that's not quite the same thing. The question is this: if I made it thoroughly well worth your while, could you pass yourself off as my wife, who was—I mean, who is—a lady? I hope you won't think me rude."

"I think you damned odd, anyway." Susie blew a puff of cigarette smoke and spoke robustly. "What's wrong with the real Sonia? Why do you want another one?"

Petticate hesitated. It seemed impossible to go further without taking Miss Smith at least in some degree into his confidence.

"As a matter of fact," he said, "my wife is dead. But it's inconvenient to me that the fact should be known—at least for a few more weeks. It's a matter of property, and insurance, and that sort of thing. Also, she's been awarded a big literary prize, and that will go west if it's discovered that she's no longer alive. But I'll explain all that later. The question is, will you try? Will you consider discussing terms?"

"Terms?" Susie looked at him with a thoughtfulness that made him feel uneasy. "Do you know, I think I rather like you?"

Petticate felt his uneasiness mount sharply. He certainly

didn't like Susie. But it equally certainly wouldn't do to let that fact slip out.

"It will be more a matter of just showing yourself than of talking and so on. But you *will* have to talk. You'll have to attend a party or two, for instance."

Susie looked interested.

"I like parties. And I don't get many of them nowadays. Life's dull, Colonel. Life's dull like you'd hardly believe. That's your strong card with me, I can tell you."

"You might get quite a lot of fun out of it." Petticate was wondering if this could possibly be true. He was also wondering, and with a good deal of dismay, whether anything could be done about Susie's accent, syntax and idiom. "Have you ever had fun before, passing yourself off as—"

"As a perfect lady?" Susie, whose interest in his proposal seemed to be mounting, cheerfully helped him out. "Oh Lord, yes. You should have seen me in India."

"India?" Petticate was surprised.

"It was usually soldiers with me, you know. Once, I tried being married to one. He was a colonel, just like you, and I was a fool not to stick to him. But it was the young majors that tempted me. I never much cared for the boys —subalterns and the like. Will you have a cup of tea?"

Since this offer appeared to involve Susie's climbing out of bed and roaming round the room, Petticate declined it hastily.

"Yes," Susie continued reminiscently, "you don't know what's your life, when you're young. Having an establishment, now. Servants and so on, like the higher-ups could turn on for you. It was crazy to turn down all that."

"That reminds me," Petticate said. "One of the first

things you will have to do is to dismiss my present servants. A married couple called Hennwife. Do you think you can manage that?"

"Goodness, yes. They'll get the right-about-turn from me, all right. If they're no good, that's to say."

"They're worse than no good. They're trying to blackmail me."

"The dirty dogs." Susie again looked thoughtful. "Do they suspect your wife is dead?"

"Yes. That's why they're going to be confounded when you turn up."

"I see." Susie's mind seemed to be working rapidly. "It looks as if we're getting to the sticky part of this. Mind your step, and no questions asked."

"Exactly." Petticate was emphatic. "That's just the basis on which I see the matter. Say three weeks, and five hundred pounds down at the end."

"Well, I don't see any reason to quarrel with that. It's a bargain, Colonel. And I won't fail you."

"I'm sure you'll do your best." Petticate offered this encouragement with genuine benevolence. "The chief difficulty will be—well, the talking. We'd better have a little practice at that."

But at this Susie Smith burst into unexpected laughter.

"Don't you worry your head about that, dearie. I know all about being the colonel's wife. You just speak in that sort of voice, and loud, and always as if you were challenging something or talking to the dog. Leave it to me."

Petticate, although somewhat disconcerted by this harsh analysis, acknowledged to himself the measure of penetration it evinced.

"Then," he said with some formality, "I will withdraw

[179]

and allow you to get up. I'll begin briefing you at lunch. No doubt Oxford has a decent hotel."

"My dear man, we catch the eleven-five to London. And you'll need about three hundred pounds. The first thing I must have isn't information about your Sonia." Susie smiled happily. "It's clothes."

It was certainly true that Susie's wardrobe was in an unsatisfactory condition. The three hundred pounds was exhausted by tea time, and in the last few shops Petticate found himself simply signing cheques. As Susie became more splendidly equipped hour by hour, the process went forward in an atmosphere of progressive obsequiousness throughout the afternoon. Petticate's dismay before all this expenditure, the necessity of which had simply not occurred to him, was mitigated by the fact that Susie was undeniably assuming gentility—a rather aggressive yet amazingly convincing gentility—with each new outward token of it that she acquired. She was ending up quite amazingly like Sonia—Sonia when some windfall from a publisher had encouraged her to go on a spree. Moreover Susie's memory seemed to be rapidly opening up upon stores of experience garnered long ago. She wasn't at all the person whom Petticate had first encountered on that train: driven back upon the lower middle-class attitudes and expedients amid which she had presumably been bred. It was hard to believe that she had ever had an auntie who had been imposed upon by a Henry Higgins, and upon whose illusory good-fortune she had herself injudiciously relied in a matter of bad cheques. Petticate reflected that the poet Kipling, who had contended in a celebrated place that Judy O'Grady and the Colonel's lady are sisters under their skins, would have felt himself notably vindicated by the present afternoon's proceedings.

Petticate himself got very little satisfaction from them. In a way he was, of course, delighted. It really did look as if this incredibly long shot could be brought off. But the very ease of the process so far was something that he found deeply disturbing. Susie's success was going to be his salvation. Yet he was going to dislike it, just as he was going to dislike her. That the thing should be possible, that a person of plebeian origins and associations should have even a chance of getting away with such a deception, was deeply mortifying to his own innate aristocracy of mind and character. What was a country coming to, one had to ask, where such things could be? Of course it couldn't *last*. Miss Susie Smith's impersonation of Mrs. Ffolliot Petticate, a woman of unchallengeably good family and breeding, could be no more than a flash in the pan—a skilfully timed flash. Even so, it was distasteful to Petticate. He looked forward to its being over.

Susie, when she had bought her last hat, decided that they must go to Fortnum's for tea. She did, Petticate reflected as he crossed Piccadilly in her wake, have a decided flair for finding her way about. From the cup of tea which he had come upon her discussing that morning to the cup of tea which she presently poured out in this gustatory paradise there yawned a chasm which she was taking entirely in her stride. There appeared to be little doubt that, if given her head, Susie would soon be enunciating with confidence such propositions as that there are no more than half a dozen places left in London in which it is possible to dine.

To Petticate, with his wide power of philosophical

generalization, there was food for thought in this. And as there was food of a more tangible order presently spread before him in pleasing variety, the succeeding half-hour became almost an agreeable one. He was turning over in his mind the rival claims of one or two delicacies which he might possibly buy on his way out through the shop, and was in consequence paying little attention to his immediate surroundings, when his ease was shattered by a single word, spoken with all too familiar vehemence from immediately behind him.

"Sonia!"

He turned round in horror. Mrs. Gotlop had just sat down at the next table. She was accompanied by the formidable old person whom he remembered to be Lady Edward Lifton. It was a moment of the most dire dismay. Susie, so far, had refused to discuss anything but clothes. She was uninstructed in the first thing that concerned the role she had to sustain.

"Darling!"

With this unhesitating exclamation Susie had risen and thrown herself into Mrs. Gotlop's arms. Mrs. Gotlop, who had also risen, embraced her and then roared with laughter.

"Back to Blimp!" Mrs. Gotlop shouted. "Back to rural Blimp!"

If Susie was baffled by this, she certainly didn't show it.

"And, *darling*," she said, "hasn't it been an *age?*"

To this Mrs. Gotlop roared a hilarious affirmative. Then she waved an arm towards her august companion.

"Of course," she said, "you know dear old Daphne?"

Susie took only a second.

"Never met Lady Edward, that I know of." Her voice was now brisk and almost cavalier. "How d'ye do?"

"How d'ye do?" Lady Edward was evidently impressed. She even favoured the false Sonia with a majestic bow.

"And now, Ffolliot, we must go." Susie had turned sharply to Petticate and motioned him to his feet. He ought, of course, already to have been standing on them, but apprehensiveness and stupefaction had frozen him where he sat. "I'm taking Ffolliot," Susie went on in what was now her best talking-to-the-dog manner, "to see his tailor. So absurd that Englishmen should be let go to their tailors alone! Asking for robbery. Never happens in Rome. Or in Madrid."

"Is that so?" Lady Edward was much impressed by this superior information, and clearly making a mental note of it for future use.

"And you will, darling, come to our next small do?" Susie had turned back to Mrs. Gotlop as she put on her gloves. "Such *ages!* I'll drop you a card. Good-bye, good-bye!" And with an expansive wave entirely appropriate in a distinguished woman of letters, Susie sailed away, leaving Petticate to make his bow to the ladies and follow her.

Out in the street, while they waited for a taxi, Petticate felt entirely limp. He had quite forgotten his delicacies. Over the way, against the railings of Burlington House, the posters were saying something about a revolution. But he didn't attend to them. He was absorbed in his recent extraordinary experience.

"Well—how did it go?" Susie had turned on him challengingly and a shade anxiously. "A sudden call, that was. Did I sound like your Sonia?"

"Not in the least. That is—yes, you must have done." Petticate found that he was far too bewildered to produce a coherent answer. "You weren't like her. You couldn't be, since you never saw her and know nothing about her. We've taken on the sheerly impossible. I see that now. I've been quite mad. And yet . . . and yet that Gotlop woman hadn't a flicker of doubt."

"*She* hadn't because *I* hadn't." Susie threw back her head and laughed, so that the commissionaire handing them to their cab glanced at her in respectful surprise. "That's psychology, dearie. If I'd flickered, she'd have flickered, and it would have been all up with us." Susie sat back with unassuming satisfaction against the dusty upholstery of the cab. "It's not knowing about your Sonia that's needed. It's nerve. And I've got nerve."

Petticate drew a long breath.

"So it seems," he said. "But you appear to have a certain amount of information, too. How did you know that old woman was Lady Edward Lifton?"

"Picture papers, silly. I've always had a fancy for turning over the society news. As for the nerve, don't think I've had it always. If I had, things wouldn't have got me down like how I was when we first met, dearie, or living like I've been doing in that nasty Eastmoor Road. No—it's something that's come back to me. And why? Because I like you, as I said." For a moment Susie was silent and thoughtful. "Queer, isn't it? You're not really very nice, I suppose. But I've quite taken to you all the same. Like some of the girls do to their ponces, I'd say. They're chaps that aren't very nice either."

It was scarcely to be expected that Petticate should produce any articulate reply to this. It was certain that, on every front, his three weeks with Susie were to be a nightmare.

"By the way," Susie went on, "tell him to drop me at

Oxford Circus."

"Drop you?" Petticate was disconcerted. "We're going to Paddington. We'll be in excellent time for the six forty-five."

Susie shook her head—and so casually that he suddenly perceived that she was a woman of iron will.

"Not for me tonight, dearie. I'll get a morning train, and we'll have a long quiet day getting up Sonia for all I'm worth. But it's a holiday for Susie Smith till then." She sighed happily. "It's been ages—it's been ages and ages—since I've been in London with a little money in my bag."

So, once more, Petticate travelled down to Snigg's Green alone. He was grateful, after all, for the break. At Paddington he bought an evening paper, simply to hide behind if any neighbours turned up. He noticed that it seemed to say something about San Giorgio. But he was so tired that he didn't bother to find out what it was.

5

During the latter part of his journey—a thing unusual with him—Colonel Petticate slept. He had been through a fantastic day—and a day which had followed immediately upon a fantastic night. No wonder he had felt quite done up. But now, as he walked slowly home from the railway station through the darkness, he found his head clearer and better able to take stock of his situation.

He had been worried about the tape recorder, buried beneath the debris of the barn. But now it occurred to him that it lay entirely within his own discretion to say whether that debris should be cleared up or not. If he simply let it all slowly disappear beneath nettles and thistles, there would probably be nobody to protest or take the slightest interest in the matter. If, at some future date, the site was cleared and the smashed machine discovered, it would be no more than a matter of a few moments' curiosity to the workmen involved. As to the rope, he must simply cut it off short where it disappeared among the masonry. Nobody pottering about in the ruins would then be remotely likely to come upon it.

No, the barn was not a problem—always provided that the Hennwifes could be sent silent and disgraced away. And there seemed to be little doubt about that. He knew just what he would do when he got home tonight. He would say crisply to Hennwife that his mistress was returning to Snigg's Green tomorrow morning. Beyond that, he would say nothing at all. The Hennwifes would be staggered by the mere statement, and the succeeding twelve hours of bewildered suspense would thoroughly unnerve them. It was very likely that at the mere sight of the false Sonia they would snatch up a few possessions and bolt. It was true they knew that he had tried to kill them. But they surely realized that they had richly deserved that fate—and only the more so since they must now believe that they had based their insolent and evil conduct upon a false assumption.

Mopping up the Hennwifes, in fact, was going to be child's play. And exceedingly agreeable child's play at that. Petticate was chuckling at the prospect when, turning a corner of the road that led past his front gate, he became aware of a stationary motor van only a few yards in front of him.

It was late for the tradesmen to be delivering anything —and moreover the van was somehow a more sombre affair than any enterprising tradesman was likely to go in for. Seized by an obscure foreboding, Petticate forced himself to take a few more paces forward. Twenty yards beyond the stationary van there was a stationary motor car. Its parking lights were switched on. And just above its roof there was an inexplicable dull blue glow.

The inexplicability lasted, of course, only for a moment. At a nearer view that dull blue glow would say "PO-LICE." And the van was a police van, too. In fact it was what, in his youth, had been vulgarly known as a Black Maria. Petticate felt a violent tremor seize and shake his frame. He wanted to turn round and run, but knew that something horrible would happen to his knees if he did. As it was, he stood transfixed, staring at his own front gate. And as he did so, he saw something stir beside it. Indeed, he saw something stir at either side of it. The gate posts might have been unnaturally moving. Only he knew that these were not gateposts but the helmets of constables—of constables who were quietly waiting . . .

And now Petticate did manage to turn round. It was to face a bright light that shone momentarily on his face, and to feel a firm grip that took him by the arm.

"All right," he heard Sergeant Bradnack's voice say. "A bit of a shock, no doubt. But just take it easy."

It was as a man in a dreadful dream that Petticate found himself led into his own hall. The Hennwifes were there, and a surprising number of policemen. Petticate stared at these policemen dully. He supposed that they must have come to turn over the rubble of the barn. The Hennwifes, it was clear, must have informed on him. They must have told of his plan to murder them, and of the fiendish manner in which they had outwitted him.

Petticate stood quite still. He didn't attempt to take off his overcoat. He supposed it was quite likely to be chilly, jolting along to jail in that black van. There was a moment's strange silence, and then Sergeant Bradnack cleared his throat and spoke.

"A very delicate matter this, Colonel. Very delicate, indeed. I have strict orders from the Superintendent to say as little as need be. But, since considerable inconvenience is going to accrue"—Sergeant Bradnack paused in some admiration over this expression—"is going to accrue to you, sir, as the employer of the apprehended persons, a word of explanation seems in place."

Petticate found himself feeling rather blindly for a chair. For seconds his physical vision was actually clouded. When it cleared, it was upon a full view of the Hennwifes. There could be no doubt about it. He had never seen them looking remotely like that before. Whatever had happened, it was something that had told them they were cornered.

"A charge of blackmail, sir, I am sorry to say. Always a very delicate matter, as you may know, sir; always a very delicate matter, indeed. The world being as it is, sir, the persons victimized don't always care to be named in court. Not by no means. And, having come forward, they deserve the protection of the law. Which is the reason, you will understand, Colonel, why I can't say much." Sergeant Bradnack paused upon this, all of which he had delivered himself of in a very loud voice. Now he suddenly leant forward and whispered loudly in Petticate's ear. "Old bastard Sir Thomas Glyde, Colonel. Nasty habits. Very nasty habits, indeed. And your precious pair got on to him."

"I see." For the first time since the rays of Bradnack's lantern had so paralysingly fallen on him, Petticate achieved articulate speech. "But I'd never have believed it—never." He looked straight at the Hennwifes. "I'd never have believed it of you," he said, sternly but sadly. "You must have been carried away, I suppose, by some sudden temptation. I am sorry—very sorry, indeed."

And now Hennwife spoke—first licking his dry lips. "Thank you, sir. I trust that you will bear witness to character, sir. I think I may say we have always endeavoured to give satisfaction."

"Yes, yes—my good fellow. I have no complaint." Petticate stood up and gave a heavy discouraged sigh. "Let us hope, Sergeant, that nothing else of a similar sort comes to light. If they proved to be anything like professional blackmailers it would of course be very much worse for them. Anything up to fifteen years."

"Quite so, sir." Sergeant Bradnack seemed a little disappointed by this turn of things. "We have naturally been wondering if they've been giving any trouble elsewhere. To yourself, for instance." Bradnack paused, as if conscious, too late, that this had not been very happily phrased. "Not in the way of attempted blackmail, of course. But perhaps the disappearance of valuables, or something of that sort."

Petticate shook his head. "No, no—they are both blameless, so far as I am concerned. But now you had better take them away, Sergeant. It's a most painful situation." Again he looked straight at the Hennwifes. "I am glad," he said, "that this didn't happen after Mrs. Petticate's return tomorrow morning. She would be deeply pained. Indeed, I shall hardly like to break it to her. Good night."

Mrs. Hennwife said nothing. Hennwife offered his employer his customary expression of thanks upon withdrawing from his presence. He even managed—although somewhat hampered by the close contiguity of the police—to back out of the front door in his established professional manner.

Petticate watched him go. He watched Bradnack and his mustered subordinates go. Then he staggered upstairs, tumbled on to his bed, drew the eiderdown over himself, and fell asleep.

6

For some hours Petticate enjoyed oblivion—if indeed oblivion can be enjoyed. And then he was assailed by dreams.

He was on the yacht with Sonia—the real Sonia—and they quarrelled. It was not the sort of quarrel that he had ever actually known with her: a measurable irritation or bad temper, bred of boredom or competing selfishness. It was the sort of quarrel for which a man stores the fuel deep in his heart—and commonly obeys a prudent instinct to keep away from. But in this dream it was suddenly a flame all around him, so that nothing seemed more natural than that he should strike at her, and strike at her to kill. That he succeeded in killing her was evident from the fact that her body as it fell to the deck shrank to the size of a dog's body—since this (Petticate knew in his dream) always does instantly happen to dead bodies. So he picked up Sonia's small dead body and threw it into the sea. Then, turning to the other side of the yacht, he saw Sonia instantly climb on board again—only this was not the true Sonia but the false Sonia, Susie Smith. Susie came out of the sea and over the gunnel and he noticed that her clothes were quite dry. He wasn't surprised by her dry crisp clothes—because he remembered that they were only acting parts in a film, and that in films actresses who have been immersed are always for some mysterious reason quite dry again a few seconds later. But he knew that he must kill the false Sonia too, and he ran at her with the boat hook. The boat hook went clean through her, so that he had to shake her body off into the sea as one shakes a dead leaf off a walking stick. He watched the false Sonia sink very slowly, as a dead leaf might sink, and then he thought how silent it was. But not entirely silent. For from somewhere behind him there came the rapid click-click of the keys of a typewriter. The sound came from the cabin. He ran towards it and looked in—and somehow it was entirely without surprise that he saw the true Sonia sitting at the machine and the keys jumping beneath her fingers. Sheets of typescript littered the cabin floor, and he thought what a pity it was that they should all be turning to pulp. They were turning to pulp because the true Sonia sat dripping wet at the typewriter, so that all the floor around her was becoming a pool and the papers were floating in it. Petticate knew that he must let out the water—for the true Sonia was now in a bath in which he had drowned her—and there was a plug to pull out which turned to a rope as he heaved, and he hoped against hope that beneath the ruins of the barn as it came tumbling down both Sonias were buried together.

The barn made a great noise as it fell. And Petticate woke up and knew that somebody was hammering at the front door.

Susie Smith had stepped back on the drive when she heard the window open almost above her head.

"Hullo!" she called. "So you're there after all. I was beginning to think it must be all a hoax. Come down and let me in."

For a moment Petticate stared at the woman in stupefaction. He had been convinced, for one thing, as he stumbled across the room, that it must still be the middle of the night. But he was looking out on broad daylight, and he realised that he must have slept until nearly noon. It was an autumn day, but Susie stood in only a short pool of her own shadow. She was surrounded by trunks and suitcases and bandboxes. She must have had all this stuff unloaded from a taxi, and then dismissed it. Petticate reflected with dismay that there could be nothing in this whole outfit for which he had not himself paid in cash or pledged credit on the previous day.

"Hullo," he said. It wasn't a usual form of greeting with him. But he could, for the moment, think of none other to utter.

"You don't sound very pleased to see me." Susie spoke with no suggestion of being aggrieved; indeed, she appeared uncommonly cheerful. "But do come and open this door. It doesn't look right, this Romeo and Juliet turn—not in an old married couple like you and me."

"I'll be down in a minute." Petticate turned round and went hurriedly to his washbasin. He had no need to dress, since he was still in the clothes—now sadly crumpled—in which he had tumbled upon his bed. But he couldn't of course go downstairs unshaved—even if some intrusive neighbour, coming up the drive, were to judge it odd that Mrs. Ffolliot Petticate should be cooling her heels outside her own front-door.

But rapid shaving didn't prove easy. His troubled night

had scarcely refreshed him, and his hand was trembling as he manipulated the razor. It was true that he hadn't been very pleased to see his substitute wife. Or rather, he had been even less pleased to see her than he had expected. He wasn't, at the moment, at all clear why this should be. He just had an obscure sense that a certain anticlimax was involved in the occasion.

The house—cold and still shuttered as he passed through it—affected him disagreeably, and he found himself fumbling with the lock that had closed automatically behind the police as they had retired with their prisoners the night before. When he did get the door open, it was to find that Susie was standing within inches of him. This was a bit of a shock.

"I've done well, haven't I?" she asked. "I got the ten-five. And guess who I travelled with."

Petticate's sense of discomfort grew. The carefree tone of Susie's voice seemed entirely genuine; and he reflected that nothing in the world builds up a woman's confidence like oceans of new clothes. At the same time she was looking at him sharply, rather as if making sure of some impression she had formed the day before.

"Travelled with?" he repeated stupidly. "No—I've no idea."

"Dear old Augusta."

"Augusta?" He stared at her. "Who is Augusta?"

"Augusta Gotlop, of course. By the way, did you know she had been a Gale-Warning?"

Petticate took a long breath. Or rather he tried to do this, out of a dim notion that it might fortify the system. It was, of course, all to the good that Susie was something of an artist. Only an artist's instinct could have carried her through that sudden crisis in Fortnum's the previous afternoon. And there were occasions in the immediate future upon which she would abundantly require this power. Nevertheless there was something alarming about it.

"Well," he said, "you'd better come in. I'll give a hand with your things."

"What about those servants?" Susie looked into the empty hall behind Petticate, evidently surprised. "They might as well make themselves useful—until I give them the sack, that is."

"You won't have to give them the sack. They've gone."

Petticate, as he said this, suddenly remembered why a sense of anticlimax was attending Susie Smith's arrival. The scene to which he had really looked forward—the confounding of the fiendish Hennwifes by a Sonia returned as from the grave—would never now take place. It didn't now *need* to take place. The Hennwife goose was otherwise cooked.

"Gone, have they?" Miss Smith took this quite casually. "Well, we can easily get more. But I'd have kept the taxi-man, if I'd known. The trunks aren't all that light. Haven't you got a chauffeur?"

"No, I always drive myself."

"I think it might be a good idea if you had a chauffeur. A chauffeur's smart, if you ask me. And Augusta has one. . . . You'd better fetch the gardener."

"There isn't a gardener. That's to say, he comes three days a week, and this isn't one of them."

Petticate, feeling understandably exasperated and also inexplicably alarmed, began ferrying suitcases into the hall. There seemed to be no end to them. Miss Smith at least didn't stand idly by. She joined in the work with gusto.

"We'll get somebody from the village to help with the trunks," she said decisively. "And of course somebody to come in and clean and wash up. I can cook for a bit; I'm really not bad at it. While you advertise." She paused, evidently remembering. "But what about that blackmail? You don't mean they've gone because you risked giving them in charge?"

"The Hennwifes are in charge, all right. And on account of blackmail. But it hasn't anything to do with me."

"I see. And will they keep mum in your direction?"

"I'm sure they will. It would be very much to their disadvantage not to. As it is"—Petticate slightly brightened as he remembered this—"they'll get a pretty stiff sentence. And quite right, too. Criminals, both of them."

"Well, it's one trouble the less, isn't it, dearie?" Susie said this in tones of the most honest cheer. "Now I think I'll have a look at my room, and then we can have a bite of lunch. I suppose there must be something in the larder?"

"At least there will be Ambrose's fish." Petticate grabbed the nearest suitcase and led the way upstairs. "Lunch, certainly," he added more graciously. "But then we have a lot to get to work on. The Hennwifes are fixed, thank goodness. But your engagement's only beginning, all the same."

Susie Smith nodded. It wasn't a statement she seemed to have any impulse to dispute.

At the top of the staircase Petticate hesitated. The Hennwifes, who alone knew which had been Sonia's actual bedroom, were gone. There appeared to be no reason, therefore, why Miss Smith should not be accommodated with some approximation to propriety in a quarter of the house remote from Petticate's own. Susie's new clothes were not immodest; indeed her particular selection from them this morning was uncannily in Sonia's manner when Sonia had been giving way to facile feelings of opulence. But Susie adequately garbed was as unmistakably a Rubens type as when she had been sitting up in bed seemingly garbed in nothing at all. It was something to which Petticate, whatever had been his tastes in the past, didn't now respond in the least—or rather responded only by feeling frightened. So this purely instinctive reaction now mingled with his habitual moral and intellectual delicacy in rendering extremely disagreeable the notion of Susie's slumbers over the next two or three weeks being divided from his own only by a single wall and an intercommunicating door.

"Your Sonia's room, of course," Susie said crisply. "I couldn't, you know, manage it from any other. The feel wouldn't be right. And the feel's the whole thing, wouldn't you say?"

Petticate, although he supposed that in fact it was, gave no audible assent to this proposition. Instead, he marched resignedly along the corridor and threw open Sonia's door.

"This is it," he said. "Of course you have your own bathroom. Through there. That other door's not in use. It's locked."

For the moment Susie didn't attend to this. She had at once walked over to the bed, sat on it, and bounced up and down critically. Petticate, who had never belonged to a world in which this sort of experimental approach to the means of repose is usual, thought for a confused moment that the action was designed to be provocative. But Susie wasn't looking at him. She was studying every aspect of the room with care.

"Yes," she said, "it's a cut above Eastmoor Road, I must say. Not, mind you, that I shan't miss the kids."

"The kids?" In a further confusion of mind, Petticate wondered whether he might have to deal with some yet undisclosed fruits of Miss Smith's unlawful loves.

"Persephone's kids, Marcus and Dominic. Still, perhaps they can come and see us some time." Susie was now prodding the pile of the carpet appraisingly with a toe. "Don't think, mind you, that I haven't known grandeur in my time."

"I'm sure you have." Petticate felt disinclined to dispute the probable quality of Susie's past professional successes. "I wonder whether there's any rearrangement you'd like?"

"Well, I won't say I don't find it a little on the dull side. Not a good exposure, if you ask me. But that blank wall, now"—and Susie pointed across the room—"what would you say to throwing out a bit of a window there? A nice bay, perhaps, with a few plants in pots. Those India-rubber ones are all the thing just now, they say. Just a suggestion, you know."

"Thank you very much." Petticate spoke flatly. He felt that he was past endeavouring to protect himself from the world with the inflexions of irony. "I'll bring up some more of those suitcases. And then we'll look in that larder."

"That's right, dearie." Susie, who had kicked off her shoes and curled her legs luxuriously under her, nodded happily. "Fish, did you say? A half bottle of Hock would be the thing. Just put it in the cold part of the refrigerator, and in fifteen minutes it will be fine." She gave a long satisfied sigh. "There's quite a lot," she said, "that I don't seem to have forgotten, after all."

If Miss Smith had forgotten little, it presently appeared that she was concerned to learn much. Before they had finished the Hock (and since Petticate had been unable to find a half-bottle they drank a whole one) there was very little she didn't know about her putative husband's affairs. Petticate hadn't meant to be nearly so communicative. There was, of course, a sense in which he was entirely in this woman's power—even more unmistakably so than he had ever been in the Hennwifes'. Even so, he had felt, it would be only prudent that she should be told as little as possible; and it had been his original intention to give her precise instructions while actually confiding to her nothing more than was absolutely necessary.

That this proposal broke down wasn't at all a consequence of Susie's bullying him. He would have resisted anything of that sort, at least for a time. The trouble— if it was to be viewed in that way—lay in Susie's intelligence. This, although untutored, was rapid. Certainly she was a good deal quicker than Petticate himself in spotting points she must be sure about. But if she saw some difficulties that his own mind hadn't got round to, this didn't seem to shake her entire confidence in her ability to sustain her deception for as long as was necessary. If she was anxious, it was about him—and indeed she was cheerfully unconcerned to conceal her feeling that he would need keeping an eye on.

Petticate didn't react too well to this suggestion that he was the weak link in the chain. There was implicit in it an assumption of his own intellectual inferiority that was naturally highly disagreeable to him. His view of the relationship in which Miss Smith would stand to him during their association had been based, he now realized, on that first impression of her gained during their brief encounter in the restaurant-car. But the present Miss Smith just wasn't that Miss Smith at all. Her temporary removal into a higher social sphere—one, it seemed, of which she had tasted a little the sweets in earlier days—had transformed the woman. And it hadn't only given her an enviable confidence. It had positively transformed her wits. Poor old Sonia had been clever in her way. It did, after all, need a certain cleverness to pour out all that stuff on the printing press. But Sonia had never had the power to run things that this woman showed. It became clearer and clearer to Petticate that there would be enormous relief in the moment at which Miss Susie Smith disappeared over his horizon for the last time.

And at least she seemed to be all for getting on with the job.

"About this San Giorgio place," she said. "Would Sonia ever have been there?"

"Not along with me. But probably she was there at one time or another. When she was younger, she put in quite a lot of time travelling around."

"I see. Well, that's not serious. What do they talk there?"

"In San Giorgio? Why, they talk Italian, of course."

"In Italy, is it? Well, I did once have ten days in a motorcoach there. Did Sonia talk Italian?"

"She talked a little. The usual thing."

"Bad accent?"

"Very bad." Petticate, who prided himself on speaking what was virtually Tuscan in a Roman mouth, was decided about this.

"Well, I can have a few phrases in a bad accent, too. It will all be pie, this Accademia Minerva business. Still, there's no point in taking risks. We'll arrive by air just before the curtain goes up, and have a date in Paris the next day. Dear old Paree."

Petticate frowned.

"You can't talk about Paree," he said. "It's an impossible vulgarism—and out of date at that."

Susie was greatly amused.

"And do you think I don't know all that stuff? But I could call it Paree to that old Lady Edward and get away with it. It's just a matter of the right air. Will you take a bet on it?"

"Certainly not. This is a serious matter."

"It's a lark, dearie. It's an enormous lark—or what would really be the point of it? What was the point of your writing that Sonia Wayward novel, if it wasn't a lark?"

"That was a matter of sober bread and butter." Petticate judged it well to keep economic realities if possible well within Susie's view. At the same time, he was struck by what she said. He was both struck and depressed by it, because it suddenly made him feel old. He *had*, after all, gone at *What Youth Desires* at least partly for a lark. But he hadn't stayed the pace. The *élan* with which he had started off had all been drained out of him by the horrors and alarms he had been through. Now, he just wanted to survive. And it was this still almost unknown female who was making all the going.

"But now about this Gialletti," Susie was saying. "He's another matter, if you ask me. That's where the tough work lies."

"Do you think so?" Petticate was rather surprised by this estimate. "It seems he never knew Sonia very well, although he talks about her in a silly enthusiastic way. All you'll have to do is to sit on a throne or whatever it's called in his studio while he chucks his clay about. You needn't even talk much."

Susie shook her head.

"Believe me dearie, if we come a cropper, it will be while that's going on. What did he like about Sonia? Not, you may be sure, just the look of her in a big vague way. I've been in on this, and I know."

"In on it?" Petticate was puzzled.

"Modelling, dearie. I once did quite a lot of it. In the altogether. And it had to be *that*, because all those painters cared about was the exact position of my navel. Unusual, it seems. I'll show you, one day." Susie paused to smile at Petticate's evident alarm. Almost for the first time, it wasn't, perhaps, a smile that was wholly kindly. "Yes, they just showed no interest in the rest of me—which wasn't how it was with gentlemen in other professions, I can assure you. It was just my navel—or perhaps I should say the way the position of that a little changed the balance of things generally. And it will be like that with this Gialletti. He'll know your Sonia's head like it was a cop with a fingerprint. It will be tough, you can take it from me."

Petticate was silent for a moment. He remembered the eminent sculptor talking his rubbish about the bones round Sonia's temples, or something of the sort. Perhaps that

[202]

wasn't just the usual pretentious thing artists did go in for. Old Gialletti, after all, was fearfully eminent. Perhaps he really would know Sonia's temples from anybody else's in the world. Perhaps—although he himself couldn't see it—Susie's temples were quite different.

"He's pretty old, is Gialletti." Petticate spoke without a great deal of conviction. "I rather got the impression that this affair of Sonia might be about his last portrait bust. He mayn't be as acute as he still thinks he is."

"We'll hope he isn't. I wonder how long he'll want?"

"I found out something about that. His usual method with these things is every day for a week, and then it's all over."

Susie considered this with more sobriety than she had as yet shown about anything.

"No use putting it off," she said. "We'd better get cracking tomorrow. Drive straight up to town, I'd say, and simply ring the bell. There's value"—Susie paused, as if seeking for an expression quite out of the ordinary— "there's psychological value in surprise. . . . And now we'll wash up."

Petticate washed up without protest. The process reminded him, more than a little nostalgically, of life on the yacht before Sonia had been so inconsiderate as to die on him and involve him in all this.

"Yes," Susie said as she put away the dishes, "we'll go by car, this time. What sort of a car do you run, dearie?"

Petticate named the highly respectable species of conveyance which had now served his needs for some years.

But Susie shook her head.

"I think," she said, "you'd better think of getting an Aston-Martin. There's a lot to be said for a touch of class."

7

Gialletti's house in Chelsea looked across the river towards Battersea Park. Or rather it didn't, on the sunny autumn morning upon which Petticate and Susie Smith arrived before it, do precisely this. The prospect was there, but the house had the air of having shut its eyes to it, since the blinds were down in all but two of the top windows.

"Perhaps they're away." Susie, standing on the doorstep, said this almost hopefully. For the first time since Petticate had renewed his acquaintance with her, she was perceptibly nervous. It was something he found himself regarding as ominous. He knew that if Susie began to fumble she would be lost. But of course it was by no means certain that she would do that. Many an actress before Susie Smith had been in a pitiable case just before putting up a superb performance. And her nervousness on this occasion did testify to her acute intelligence. She was undoubtedly right—Petticate had concluded upon reflection—in seeing the business with Gialletti as her supreme test.

"Try another ring," he said. "There may be nobody about except Gialletti himself, and he may be buried in his studio."

Susie tried another ring. It had no effect in securing

any attendance upon the front door, but it was presumably the occasion of a window at the top of the house being thrown violently open. An elderly woman thrust her head through it with an air of some indignation.

"*A lei suonato?*" she shouted.

"Certainly we rang." Petticate thought the question plainly superfluous. And he was reluctant to begin bellowing Italian in a London street. "Is Mr. Gialletti at home?"

"*Il signore e partito. Partiremo presto. Viva la liberta!*" The woman waved her hands. She appeared to be in a high state of excitement.

"Then isn't there anybody at home?"

"*La scala secondaria.*" The elderly woman made a large circular gesture, and banged down the window.

"How extremely uncivil," Petticate said.

"An Italian, was she? You can't expect them to behave like we do." Susie offered this pacifically. "But what did she say?"

"She appeared to suggest that we should find another staircase at the back."

"Then round we go. The studio may be in a mews, or something like that." Susie glanced along the street. "Along there, I think."

It proved to be a good guess. At the back of the house there was a building which must at one time have sheltered carriage, horses and coachman. It was now rather lavishly and artily got up—in a manner, however, seeming to date from a good many years back, when Gialletti had been fashionable rather than eminent.

"That's it," Petticate said, and pointed to an affair like a crane that protruded from an upper aperture. "I suppose they hoist up his chunks of marble with that."

[205]

"I don't see any way of getting in." Susie studied the building. "Oh, yes—up that outside staircase. It lets you in right at the top."

They climbed, and came to a door that was ajar. There was no bell or knocker, but in the middle was a small and tarnished brass plate saying "Gialletti." Petticate thumped on the wood and got no reply, although there was some suggestion of sound and movement from inside.

"Better walk in," Susie said. She seemed quite to have recovered her nerve. "I'd say it's what's intended— wouldn't you?"

They walked in, and found themselves at once in an open gallery, and looked down into a vast studio filled with a cold clear light that fell through correspondingly vast northward-facing skylights. Curtains, tapestries and a rolled-up carpet suggested considerable luxury, but the whole place was clearly in process of being closed down. A row of packing cases along one wall appeared intended to take a collection of large and middle-sized bronzes stacked on the floor. Indeed it looked as if nothing was intended to stay put except several masses of marble so huge and amorphous that they had the appearance of geological phenomena which some seismic disturbance had thrust up through the floor of the studio. Or they might have been icebergs, for they gave the whole place a decidedly chilly look. Yet it wasn't, in fact, chilly. It was, on the contrary, rather hot.

At the far end of the studio was a large stove. It was alight and blazing fiercely. This accounted for the temperature. Petticate saw that it was being used simply for the rapid disposal of piles of miscellaneous rubbish. He was just taking in this fact with some perplexity when there was a clanking sound immediately underneath him, and a young man appeared from below the gallery. He was shoving a wheelbarrow piled with litter, and for a moment it looked as if he were entirely naked. Petticate —and certainly Susie, who gave a squeak of pleasure— had remarked a golden torso, and a ripple of muscle under a fine skin, before it became apparent that the owner of these attractive attributes was at least wearing some very short shorts.

"Hullo!" Susie called out. "Please, may we come down?"

The young man dropped the handles of his barrow, turned round, and looked up at the gallery.

"Oh, I say, Mrs. Petticate—what tremendous fun!" The young man, having produced this greeting without a second's hesitation, turned a more formal, but still frank and pleasing, regard upon Mrs. Petticate's husband. "Good morning, sir. You won't know me, but I'm Timmy Gialletti. How nice of you to drop in. Won't you come downstairs?"

They found an inside staircase and descended it. Petticate, a good deal shaken by his sudden immersion in the world of *What Youth Desires*, found it necessary to resist a tendency positively to grope his way. He had entirely forgotten the existence of this young man, whose acquaintance Sonia must have gained when making a professional study of the Giallettis from the life. Of Timmy, indeed, such a study might rather be called from the nude; and Petticate wondered whether some morbid strain of exhibitionism was perhaps in question.

"I'm so sorry to appear like this." Timmy smiled charmingly, grabbed a chair that was lying overturned beside

[207]

the wall, dusted it deftly with the palm of a hand, and presented it to Susie. "The fact is, I'm shoving a good deal of stuff around, and this is how I have the habit of doing it." He turned to Petticate. "I couldn't by any chance," he asked blandly, "interest you in five tons of a very tolerable Carrara marble? It would be a standby for years—whenever, I mean, aunts and uncles and so-forth passed away."

Susie laughed unrestrainedly at this. "Isn't Timmy"— she gave his naked upper arm a skittish pat that froze Petticate's blood—"just too droll?"

"We have come, as you may guess, to call on your father." Petticate preserved a decent cordiality, but sought to show that he was disposed to get down to business. "There are sittings to arrange for the bust he is to undertake of my wife. I think you will have heard of it."

"Oh, yes—but of course." For a moment Timmy Gialletti appeared almost at a loss. "My father wanted to execute it very much, very much indeed. He will be"— Timmy hesitated, and then chose a word that came plainly from the paternal vocabulary—"he will be desolated. But I suppose you haven't heard the news?"

"The news?" Petticate was extremely disconcerted. He couldn't square either Timmy's words or manner with the first notion that had come into his head: namely, that the great sculptor must be dead.

"The revolution in San Giorgio, sir. Of course you may have missed it. The splash in the papers isn't anything very much. But it's the supreme event of my father's life. He's been working for it for years."

"But how marvellous!" Susie's utterance was a gasp of admiration and joy. Her Anglo-Indian background, it appeared, was unexpectedly blended with republican fervour.

"The old man's been pouring money into the revolutionary underground for years. And now it's paid off. He left for San Giorgio by air last night. The whole household—they're mostly Italians, of course—are following today. But I'm staying behind myself. You see, I feel entirely English. And, as a matter of fact, I shall soon be marrying an English girl."

"I congratulate you." Petticate's correct demeanour did not desert him in face of this confusing situation. "And your father will no doubt be—um—a moderating influence upon the rebels. Not that I use that word in any derogatory sense."

Timmy Gialletti laughed. "Well, sir, they're not rebels any longer now. There's no doubt that the *coup* has been a complete success, and that the new men are firmly in the saddle. My father, of course, is going to be first President."

"But how perfectly splendid!" Susie's enthusiasm grew. "Do you think he will be willing to receive old friends? How much Ffolliot and I would *love* to dine with the President of *darling* San Giorgio! Wouldn't we, my poppet?"

"Oh—most certainly." Petticate only felt that Susie must at all costs be got away. "No doubt in the circumstances," he went on, "the bust your father has been so anxious to execute of Sonia will have to wait."

"Well, yes." Timmy Gialletti's delightful features once more seemed to admit a tinge of embarrassment. "In fact —well, definitely. I'm terribly afraid it will seem like a broken promise. But it's really a matter of religion—or *almost* of religion. The fact is, my father has taken a sort of vow. In thanksgiving for the deliverance of San Giorgio from a century of tyranny, and so forth. The entire energies of his life are now to be devoted to a colossal memorial to the heroes of the revolution. *Really* colossal. The marble, you know, won't have so far to come. How I can see him making the chips fly! I expect I'll go out and give him a hand, now and then. It's surprisingly good exercise, when you can't row."

"I'm very, *very* disappointed," Susie said. "But I always thought your father was a dear. And—shall I tell you something, Timmy? Ffolliot won't mind, I know. I think you're a dear, too."

The Petticates—as it might be reasonable to call them—set off for Snigg's Green largely in silence. Petticate himself was aware that in Susie Smith the unexpected issue of their expedition had induced a conflict of emotions. She was relieved, just as he was himself. But she was also disappointed as he decidedly was not. It came down, no doubt, to a difference of temperament. He, being entirely the rational and prudent man, had no relish for unnecessary risks. The necessary ones were harassing enough, in all conscience. But Miss Smith—there was no denying it—was an artist, and it had been in the great Gialletti's studio that she had believed herself destined to bring off the supreme thing. She would rejoice in the turn she was to put on before the Accademia Minerva. But, because easier, it would be less satisfactory.

Petticate, although his own mind didn't work at all in this way, was conscious of having, although very obscurely, certain feelings of dissatisfaction himself. It was puzzling, because his perplexed situation was really resolving itself very nicely. The Hennwifes had turned out to be no danger at all; as a menace they had unexpectedly collapsed—and without even the necessity of confronting them with the false Mrs. Petticate. And now it had been much the same with Gialletti. Petticate's horizons were clearing rapidly. And yet he wasn't, for some reason he couldn't fix, entirely happy about it all.

They had lunch in Oxford, where Susie had decided she must take the opportunity of seeing Marcus and Dominic. She spoke of them—she really seemed to contrive to think of them—as parts of a remote past for which she from time to time nostalgically yearned. Petticate judged this silly, and he certainly didn't propose to accompany her to Eastmoor Road—to which her return indeed, while briefly enjoying the handsome outer trappings of Mrs. Petticate, struck him as being in dubious taste. But he did feel that he deserved a good luncheon, and that he could enjoy a quiet cigar afterwards, while Miss Smith went about her tiresome occasion. He wondered how she would explain to the children's parents the sudden and obtrusive change in her fortunes, and whether she had it in mind simply to return to her former dwelling, the richer by £500, when her present adventure was concluded.

The lunch at least was satisfactory—and would have been more so but for a certain solicitousness in Susie as to what he should eat and drink that struck him as being entirely without appropriateness to their situation. It was a quite vast relief when she left him for an hour. Not that he then ceased to be conscious of her. Though she was no longer with him in the flesh—that abounding flesh which he had to acknowledge himself positively repelled by—she remained a problem to brood over. Susie

Smith had, he supposed, a suppressed maternal instinct as well as an uninhibited and cheerful acquisitive one. The combination was peculiarly disagreeable to him.

They got home by tea-time. Susie insisted on stopping in the village and going into the baker's. Petticate, waiting impatiently in the car, could see her gossiping happily with the baker's wife behind the counter. As far as the business of being Mrs. Ffolliot Petticate was concerned, this could only be reckoned as a very minor turn. But Susie emerged from it quite cheered up. She put down a paper bag on the seat between them.

"Crumpets for today," she said. "And muffins for tomorrow."

Petticate received this grumpily.

"Please yourself," he growled as he started up the engine. "At tea-time I never eat anything except shortbread biscuits."

"Then wait." Susie was out of the car again in an instant, and this time she returned quite quickly, carrying a tin. "From Edinburgh," she said. "I once lived there. It was with a very nice Major. And I learnt just what shortbread to ask for. Alex—that was my Major's name —used to love it, too."

To this trivial reminiscence Petticate made no reply. He was noticing that the quality of his uneasiness had changed. Foreboding would have been the better word for it now.

It was certainly under the influence of this feeling that Petticate, after tea, and hard upon wiping the last crumbs of shortbread from his moustache, grabbed the telephone and called up Wedge. There was now, after all, only one major crisis ahead, and the sooner he got a grip on it the better. Sonia Wayward must turn up for her prize. After that—only provided that Petticate benefited from past experience to arrange matters more skilfully this time—she could vanish as a physical entity, as distinct from a creative mind, once and for all. In other words this tiresome Susie Smith could go one way, and Petticate himself with his portable typewriter would go another. The novel writing would be a terrible bore. But, with only himself to provide for in inexpensive but agreeable parts of the world, he need not labour at his curious future livelihood too often.

After some irritating palaver with a subordinate, he got through.

"Wedge? Petticate speaking."

"Oh . . . you."

Petticate, although he was unable to judge this at all civil, continued to endeavour after a cordial tone.

"I have a piece of news for you, my dear fellow. Sonia is home."

"Well?"

Petticate frowned over the instrument. He supposed it must be defective.

"Can you hear me?" he asked. "Shall I insist on another line? I said that Sonia is home."

"I can hear you perfectly well. You said that Sonia is home. What about it?"

This time, Petticate was really alarmed. There was an odd quality in Wedge's voice that the Postmaster-General certainly wasn't to blame for.

"Dash it all, Wedge—that prize. The Golden Nightingale, or whatever it's called. We can fix up the arrangements now."

This produced no articulate reply. It did however produce a noise that Petticate found entirely perplexing.

"What was that?"

"What was that? It was a howl of rage, Petticate. And now can you hear me grinding my teeth?"

"My dear chap, stop fooling." Petticate said this without conviction. There was now no mistaking the fact that Wedge was in a singularly bad temper.

"Fooling? And who the devil is fooling, if it isn't yourself? Haven't you heard of the revolution in San Giorgio? There won't be any more prizes. There won't be any more Accademia Minerva. It's been dissolved. After all, the whole thing was just publicity for their rotten casinos and things, wasn't it? And the new government is far too high-minded for all that."

"But this is outrageous!" Petticate himself was now near to gibbering with rage. "Think of their new President! Gialletti himself. A man who is a great admirer of my wife's books."

"Rubbish, Petticate. You mean your wife's bones—and he's far too busy to bother his head about them now. You don't think that an artist like Gialletti—a thorough highbrow after your own heart—could really admire Sonia's tripe? The idea's just silly. And, by the way, have you any notion of how many copies of *What Youth Desires* I've had printed? Have you any notion of how much money I'm going to drop now that the whole stunt's off? If it doesn't mean bankruptcy, it means something damned near it."

For some moments Petticate, assaulted in this way, could find no words. His mind was in a most pitiable confusion.

Much of what Wedge had told him he now realized that he might reasonably have guessed at. His chief difficulty appeared to be in deciding whether the news was good or bad. On the one hand it meant a very considerable sum of money going west. But on the other hand it represented the disintegration and disappearance of the last remaining crisis in his affairs—of what was, in fact, already the sole surviving occasion of his bringing his wife spuriously back to life again. This thought did presently prompt him to speech.

"But, look here," he said—and was aware of his own incoherence as he spoke. "Look here, Wedge—what am I to do about Sonia?"

"*Do* about her? Good Lord, man—do as you please. Pack her off again to the Bermudas, or wherever it was. If we're to judge by *What Youth Desires* she does her stuff the hell of a lot better there than when living at your blessed Snigg's Green." The bad temper had by no means departed from Wedge's voice. "Buy her a tropic isle somewhere, and make a yearly trip in that yacht of yours to collect the latest manuscript. We'll have to think again, by the way, about changing that sliding scale. Goodbye."

Petticate put down the receiver, left his study, and walked like a man in a dream to the drawing-room—which was the apartment in which Susie Smith had established herself. She had cleared away the tea things and was sitting by the fire. And she was knitting.

It was the knitting, somehow, that unnerved Petticate most. Susie might have been a *tricoteuse*, waiting to see him go rolling past on a tumbrel.

"I've been talking to Wedge," he said. "The whole business in San Giorgio is off. The revolution has killed it."

"You mean we don't go?"

"Just that. Certainly we don't go."

"But what a shame!" Susie was genuinely upset. "All that fun of being Sonia Wayward and getting a prize from a prince gone down the drain because of a stupid revolution! I looked forward to that, I did. And you'd have loved hobnobbing with royalties." Momentarily and for the first time, Susie looked thoroughly dejected. Then she brightened and laid down her knitting. "Never mind," she said. "Let's cheer ourselves up, dearie. Let's have a party."

"A party?" Petticate was merely bewildered.

"Drinks. And just by ringing round. That's much the nicest way. I'll begin with Augusta."

"Augusta?" To Petticate the name seemed to do no more than ring the faintest of bells.

"Who was a Gale-Warning. Augusta Gotlop. And do you think Lady Edward would come? We'll ask some others, and you'll tell me all about them first. It will be our next big lark."

Petticate had gone quite pale. "I must point out—" he began.

"But there's one other thing—before the post goes. The advertisement for *The Times*."

"The advertisement for *The Times*?" Quite unconsciously, Petticate had got out a handkerchief and was mopping his brow.

"For servants. We can't go on doing all our own skivvying, dearie."

"I suppose we could—for the fortnight or three weeks that it looked as if you would have to remain here. But, as it is, your engagement"—Petticate advanced this word boldly—"is really at an end already. Come to think of it, you haven't been necessary at all." He laughed an insincere and hideous laugh. "As things have fallen out—first about the Hennwifes, and then about this whole Gialletti and San Giorgio business—I need never have invented you."

She was looking at him with amusement.

"But you have, dearie. And here I am."

"Yes, of course." Petticate contrived some grotesque travesty of genial response. "And you did well, and you'd have continued to do well, I'm sure. But it's all over. And I'll get you that £500 tomorrow."

For a moment Susie seemed to consider this seriously. Then she took up her knitting again.

"Of course that was the arrangement, dearie. But it wouldn't do. It wouldn't do for *me*. I couldn't bear to leave you—not now. And it isn't just that things look like being very comfortable here." Susie paused in her knitting to look appreciatively round the room. "It's certainly very nice. There's a touch of class to it that comes natural to me, as you can see. And I'll like that room upstairs—the one next to yours, that is—once we get the new window thrown out. But that's all on the side, as I say. The real thing is that I don't want to leave *you*." Susie paused again —this time to gaze at Petticate with perfect sincerity. "Of course you're a bit of a low hound. There's no denying it. But I've taken a fancy to you."

During most of this speech, Petticate had stood as if petrified before an approaching doom. But now he did manage to begin to speak.

"If you think that *I've* taken—"

"And it wouldn't do for you, dearie. You may think it would but it wouldn't. Ffolliot Petticate without Sonia Wayward—a real live Sonia Wayward, at bed and board, as they say—just wouldn't work. You'd begin to slip at once, my boy. And you'd be far down the hill within a year."

There was a long moment's silence. Petticate's absolute dismay before what he had heard was only deepened by a lurking knowledge that this fatal woman's words held some grain of horrible truth.

"You really imagine," he asked with feeble sarcasm, "that you can take Sonia's place *for good?* I suppose you think you can even write her novels?"

Susie laughed easily.

"We know who can do that, dearie. And I think, by the way, you should be able to manage two a year. At least for a good time ahead, that is. It's just a matter—isn't it?— of regular hours. And it will be worth it. We might have that Aston-Martin in no time. And now I'll go and ring up Augusta."

And Susie got up and left the room. Petticate watched her go. It was her mere way of moving, somehow, that set the seal on the thing as inevitable. She was—nobody could question it for a moment—the long-established mistress of the house. Weakly, unprotestingly, Petticate sank into a chair. The rest of his life, he saw, was to be lived, in more sense than one, under the shadow of the New Sonia Wayward.

[218]